SnowShine's Story

Chapter One
My Name Is SnowShine

Hello everyone. My name is SnowShine. I guess you have probably never heard of me. I am too small to be noticed. You see, I am an elf. Not an important elf. Nobody ever talks about me. I am not like Rudolph the famous reindeer, or Frosty the famous snowman, or everyone's *favourite* favourite, Father Christmas. I am just one of Santa's many elves.

In fact the only important thing about me, if you could call it important at all, is that I am very small. Even for an elf. I am in fact the smallest, easiest-not-to-notice elf in Santa's kingdom. At least...I used to be.

This is a story about an adventure that happened one Christmas not so long ago – the sort of 'not so long ago' that makes me unsure if, in your human time, it has already happened or is it about to happen soon.

Santa had been busy all year, as usual, reading mail from children and making toys. From the children's letters – brought by his elves

GobDrop
and
SnowShine

by

Adrian Beckingham

First published by Mogzilla in 2013

ISBN: 9781906132538

Copyright © 2013 Adrian Beckingham
Cover art and illustrations by Jason Smith
www.macaruba.com

Cover and layout copyright © Mogzilla 2013
Edited by Mogzilla.

www.mogzilla.co.uk

Printed in the UK

that wander the world — Santa realised that people were feeling less happy than usual that year. People were worrying about not having enough money for presents.

We elves do not understand what all the fuss is about this strange stuff called money.

We make toys and give them to Santa, and he gives them to children all over the world. The best toys go to the best-behaved girls and boys. The Naughty List makes sure of that, doesn't it?

Call us daft, but we don't do things for money. We like to give just for the joy of giving.

Anyway, we kept hearing news of how little money the humans had now, and we wondered where had it all gone? None of us knew. Not even Santa.

Santa did not want people to be sad. He decided he must do something special to help people rediscover the joy in their hearts. Then one day he opened a letter from a young girl called Crystal.

Crystal wrote that rather than a present under her tree, she would love to wake up and have Father Christmas sing her a Christmas song as her special present.

Of course! The joy of Christmas songs! Santa roared with laughter. Why hadn't he thought of it himself? What better than a merry Christmas song, sung by Santa himself, to cheer everyone up? Best of all singing is a pleasure that does not cost money.

Santa set to work, remembering as many traditional Christmas songs as he could.

As each song bubbled forth he would practice it, and once he was happy he could sing it properly, he set it aside.

Soon the shelves in his workshop were glistening with freshly polished songs, and Santa wondered what to do to keep them from spilling everywhere. So he asked his elves to make a magic bag to put them in.

Elves can weave and thread light better than anyone – and the bag they wove for the songs was red like the flames of the fire, and covered in stars that shone as gold as the sun.

Santa was delighted, and soon that bag was swelling as it hummed and whistled away. Then Santa decided to search for some new songs for his collection. He said to his elves:

"Go out into the world and search for Christmas songs. Long ones, short ones, fast ones and slow ones, bendy ones and bouncy ones, but most of all merry ones. Rock'n'roll, hip-hop, classic songs and new ones. Borrow all the songs you can find!"

Then Santa gave a wink and added:

"People won't know that their songs are missing, as we will use an Elf Invisibility spell to cover it up. But my elves, be sure to take each and every song back to its owner before Christmas Eve."

So that is exactly what the elves did. They set out from the North Pole and, using magical skills at being *ever so* quiet and *ever so* unseen, they took that empty bag of Christmas songs and slowly began to fill it up.

Now the bag does not look big because it was made by elven hands. But the inside of the bag is much much bigger than the outside.

This is just as well because the elves had to carry it down chimneys and along drainpipes and over garden walls. They bashuffled and they shamringled through the windows and doors of people's homes, concert halls, schools and libraries and galleries, car parks and skyscrapers – searching for Christmas songs to take back to Santa.

Each time they found one, they would load it into the bag of Christmas songs, and then fold a small pocket of time and space so that no one could tell it was gone. When the bag was bulging with music, they sent it back to Santa.

The elves had plenty of time, or so they thought, before the songs would ever be missed. Christmas still seemed ages away.

So there were all the elves – at least all the more important, bigger ones, everyone except me – heading off from Santa's Lodge to find songs, and bringing them back to add to his bag of Christmas songs. How happy everyone was, alive with the joy of the songs. All the elves and animals sang together while they worked.

The elves had other work to get on with, of course. There was all the usual stuff we do year in and year out, like peeking at children's good and naughty habits, and making sure luck is on a child's side whenever we can. As the year rolls on we collect lists of who has been good, who has been naughty and who has wished for what as their special Christmas gift.

Misbehaving children. That's what we elves are told to look out for. But misbehaving, as it happens, is something that I do myself.

You see, I *so* wanted to go out into the world. Everyone else was doing it. Why couldn't I? Whenever I asked, the other elves just smiled, and said: "SnowShine, you are *too* small. You are not ready for the world yet. You will see everything once you have grown up a bit."

Now how do you think that made me feel? I was sad. I mean, even though I am small, I have the same sized feelings as everyone else.

To try to make me feel better they gave me a task that was mine and mine alone – unraveling tangled Elven Thread.

Elven Thread is the bendiest, stretchiest, strongest, shammmooooozeliest binding in the world. Forget about you humans with your super-strong steel. Forget about spider webs. Or Goblin String. I once saw some elves stretch a tiny piece of Elven Thread. It started off no longer than my thumb – they wrapped it ten times around Santa's Great Hall, and still it had not snapped.

The more you pull and stretch Elven Thread, the stronger it becomes. But sometimes it can tangle. And when it gets tangled up, nothing on earth can untie it. Nobody but me. You see I, Santa's Smallest Elf, have a talent for that one task.

To most elves those tangles look like troubles. To me they look like puzzles. It's a bit like life, which sometimes can seem a terrible muddle can't it? Everything seems so confused and twisted about. But every tangle can be unraveled. If you just know where to begin pulling, it all slides out nice and orderly again.

One day, when everyone was out and about or too busy to notice me, I suddenly had a silent and rather naughty thought. I could creep off and take a peek at the world. It was all just beyond these walls... the rolling mountains covered in ice and snow, the enormous frozen bergs of looming white. Penguins, seals, and walruses.

To the sounds of banging hammers, clasping tongs, striking anvils, burrowing chisels and sploshing paintbrushes, I walked along the echoing corridor away from the Toy Room.

Elves were here and elves were there, elves were everywhere, rolling out long paper lists and reading children's wishes from them. The sounds of wooden screwdrivers and popping springs echoed busily down the hallway.

The further I walked the fewer elves I saw and the fainter those echoes became until they were only a soft hum. I followed the corridors, turning this way then turning that. Now you might think some bigger elf might ask me, Santa's Smallest Elf, what I thought I was doing wandering about all alone? But I guess they hardly noticed me, for they were all so busy. A few did look up as I passed, but I tried my best to smile and look official.

Of course, I had walked along these corridors to Santa's door before. I had even gone for walks with my elf mother and father, exploring the forest and skating on frozen lakes. But never very far from Santa's Lodge.

My parents and all the bigger elves told me that to go out alone was not being careful. They told me that hungry tiger seals were hunting in the water, and that even hungrier polar bears were roaming the snowy plains.

So as I rounded the next corner and found myself standing there, staring up at the towering door to Santa's Lodge, I stopped and wondered what I was doing. Would you stretch up on your tip toes and open that huge door to the looming wilderness outside?

I tried, but the door handle was just too high. I needed something to make me taller. I was used to this problem. I peered this way and that and saw a stool. It was made of solid crystal, forged over thousands of years in the belly of the earth, glittering with light. It probably belonged to Santa, or one of the big elves. These stools were never made for anyone as small as me. I was never even allowed to sit on one.

How do you think I moved that enormous stool to the door? By pushing it? No way, it was too heavy by far. By pulling? Nope. By sliding? By turning it over and rolling it? No. It was far too heavy to budge, remember. I used Elf Dust.

Elf Dust is a tool like brooms or Hoovers are to you humans. It can make nearly anything turn to gas. The only thing I know that can resist it is Elven Thread, which can withstand anything. The better the grade of Elven Dust, the longer it lasts.

As Santa's Smallest Elf I get the lowest grade of Elf Dust – Y Grade. But it still turns almost anything to mist, even if only for a few moments. I checked my pockets. I only had one pinch left. Not to worry, my parents would give me more. Would you use your last bit of Elf Dust to move a heavy stool?

I sprinkled the stool's legs with Elf Dust and a cloudy mist rose in front of me. All I had to do was fill my lungs with air, and blow. The stool drifted over to the door. Moments later it began to drip like a wax candle, and it became a solid crystal stool again.

Now you might wonder why I didn't just sprinkle the Elf Dust on the door itself, to save all this trouble? But the door to Santa's Lodge is magic proof, nothing gets in, and nothing gets out, unless by conventional means. Like ringing the huge shiny golden doorbell *ting aling aling ting ting* and being invited in. Or turning the handle and walking out. Easy.

Easy? Oh yes? Not when you're as small as me, and you are leaving without permission. I grabbed one of the crystal legs and climbed it like a tree to the top, clinging on tight with my hands and knees and sliding myself up like a caterpillar. I managed to reach the handle, and I hung from it with my legs kicking. The handle groaned, sighed and then flicked downwards. The floor looked a pretty long way down, as I slipped off and went somersaulting down.

But I am no heavy footed human. I can twist and pirouette in the air better than a cat. We don't keep cats at Santa's Lodge, by the way. They would eat us or tease and terrify us with their sharp claws. What we keep at Santa's Lodge instead are white rabbits, or Arctic hares to be precise. Their fur is soft and warm, and it glows so brightly that they can hide just by standing still in the white snow. They are wise, kind, and often brave.

Anyway, so there I was somersaulting through the air. I landed nimbly on my feet.

The Door swung open, and immediately the blinding light of the snow dazzled my eyes. With a deep breath and beating heart I stepped out of Santa's Lodge and set off into the snows of the North Pole.

Chapter Two
The Ice Mountains

I gasped. It was such a beautiful day outside – very cold, but with a golden light in the sky, and shimmering snow as far as I could see. Standing at the doorway to Santa's Lodge I could see a very tall iceberg mountain. How I had always wished I could climb it! If I climbed that ice mountain, I thought, I could look down on everyone else and instead of being Santa's Smallest Elf, I'd be The Tallest Elf Of Them All.

That had always been a dream of mine. All the biggest elves had very busy schedules. They had no time for someone as little as me.

I met one once – one of the biggest elves that is. One day I was there unravelling a chaotic ball of Elven Thread, when I saw a bustling bunch of self-important elves scurrying along in my direction. I had to lean right in against the curve of the tunnel and breath in tight so as not to get stomped on as they rushrumbled along. Then I gasped, for behind them was the biggest elf I had ever seen – I mean he must have been half as tall as Santa himself, and that is megabustingly huge for an elf. He had all these servants before him who had bumblerimbled me to the side, and he passed without even noticing me.

Then came more servants following behind, all chumbingaling and carboodling along in a frenzy of tinsel and scissors and shining paper and cotton balls and wax.

It turned out that they were looking for me. Ten miles of Elven Thread had become awfully knotted in the Toy Room. Ten miles. Who can unknot that? SnowShine, that's who. So off I went to help. But not one of them said thanks. They were much too important for that.

Do you think it's important to say thanks when someone helps you, no matter how much smaller or less important they may seem to be? Well these elves forgot. I didn't mind. I was used to that.

Well that was ages ago, but stood here at Santa's Door I glanced behind me. Would anyone miss me if I left for a short while? Me – the smallest elf of all? Off to climb a mountain to feel like The Tallest Elf Of Them All. Miss me? Surely not. But was it safe to go? The white landscape stretched out in every direction, full of hills and valleys and wide frozen plains, and right at the edge of the world, it seemed, that tall fist of ice mountain that reached higher than anywhere else. I thought of the Arctic wolves and my heart beat faster. Was I really going to do this?

So I set off crossing the ice and snow. It took a long time. It was a hard climb, with slippery paths and steep drops everywhere. But I am an elf, after all, and we are very clever with ice and melting snow, so in the end I made it. One moment I was still huffing and puffing, sliding across ice craters and slamming into piles of snow. And the next, one step, two steps, and there I was. At the top of the tallest ice mountain I had ever seen.

Wow! The world looked great from up here. Far behind me, I could see the glint of the tall tower that stands high above Santa's Lodge.

The tower is very tall, very bright, but so thin and fine it cannot be seen by humans.

There is so much that humans can't see. Everything we see is reflections of colour and light, and human eyes can only see 1 out of every 1000 colours. That means humans can't see 999 real things for every one real thing they do see. Can you believe that? We elves know it's true, and we use it to slide into the shades that are beyond human sight, and make ourselves invisible.

Anyway, there I was looking out towards The tower over Santa's Lodge and the long sweeping landscape, when I turned around and what did I see there ahead of me? Another ice mountain. Taller than this one.

I gulped. And then I set off. I wanted to be atop the highest mountain of all. To stand on top of the world.

Down I went, and up I went. To the top of the iceberg. And there ahead of me was... a taller ice mountain.

I began my slide down the slope, bouncing along the icy pathways and skimming across frozen lakes. Humans cannot do these things. At least, well, some humans can — they even hold competitions I hear — but they are heavier than elves. Humans are so heavy they would fall through the sort of ice we elves skate on. And of course I am Santa's Smallest Elf. Even thin ice that has barely frozen can hold me.

As I climbed the next mountainous iceberg, a storm whipped up. The air was filled with thick bolts of snow. Icy wind was blustering this way and that. I could not see. I stumbled about and when the storm cleared, I had lost my way.

Chapter Three
The Cave Of The Goblin

So there I was, lost in the ice mountains, not knowing which way to go. In every direction I saw high frozen walls all around me.

I do not know what awful things might have happened to me if I had not been found. Perhaps I would still be stood in one spot under a pile of fallen snow, or I might have been gobbled up by a polar bear or a tiger seal. But something even more horrid happened to me.

There I was, lost and cold, when suddenly I was spotted by someone who lived there all alone among those snowy peaks. Give me those wild bears or Arctic wolves any day! It was GobDrop the Christmas Goblin who found me.

I am sure you have heard of him. No? Well soon everyone will know his name. He is a legend at Santa's Lodge. We elves know everything about him, except where he lives. But the stories we could tell. GobDrop does not like Christmas songs. He does not like Christmas trees, Christmas food or Christmas presents.

GobDrop hates Christmas. All of it. Every year. And the worst thing he ever did? He stole The Naughty List. Now, I had heard lots of stories about GobDrop. Snuggled up nice and warm beside one of the many roaring fires in Santa's Lodge, I had heard about the big black circles of hair around GobDrop's eyes, about the shiny yellow fur coating his sharp unbrushed teeth, and about the click clack of his nasty claws. And I remember the big elves that sat there telling me about GobDrop as we sat round a warm flickering fire, saying how his horns were the most terrible thing about him. "Horns?" I had asked. Sitting snugly on a warm knee. "Are they like reindeer horns? That sounds very grand."

But the big elf just said:

"Nope, not grand at all. Just hideous. GobDrop has horns like an enormous EtoFier."

EtoFiers are one of those things humans just can't see or hear. You can walk right through them and not even know they are there. Which is lucky for you. I suppose you would say that they are a bit like lizards, only these lizards are the size of giraffes with the armour of a rhino. And horns that can pierce right through the trunks of trees, and as soon as an EtoFier's horn goes through you, you turn into dust. Why, the only creatures that terrify me more than EtoFiers are ShuffleBelches: enormous blind and deaf worms that hunt by vibration, feeling you as you walk, even a hundred miles away.

They burrow below the ground before coming up and eating you from below. Some are so huge they are said to swallow whole houses full of elves or dwarves in a single gulp.

But the only thing that terrifies me even more than ShuffleBelches is GobDrop the Christmas Goblin: the meanest creature in the North Pole.

I had trembled with fear when I had first heard the stories about GobDrop, as I sat beside the flickering fire. But here in the shimmering white wilderness, when I saw GobDrop himself high on the mountain slope above me, I knew what real fear was.

I saw him come lumbering down the snowy hill, springing on his powerful legs. His legs were long and hairy like spider's legs, but he only had the two of them. He came boomfangering straight toward me down that steep slope with a glimmer in his cold eyes. He shamroozled down that white hillside and punched at the air with his fists, then did a quick but really high somersault and landed firmly on his two hairy feet.

I tried to hide behind a tree, as I watched his body shift this way and that, through the snow. He was covered in patches of purple and green, and his torso was thick with shaggy long fur. The claws on his feet were long and sharp. I heard the frozen ground gasp in a screech each time those ghastly claws sliced into the ice.

But there was one thing that I did notice. It surprised me despite my dread. He had no horns. His horns were meant to be the worst thing about him. Had the elves been wrong in how they had described him, or was this not GobDrop at all, but some other foul creature?

I tried to stay as quiet as I could, hiding behind a tree, but the goblin didn't need his eyes to see me. I peeked out from my hiding place and there he was, twitching his long goblin nose and smelling me out.

I squished up as small as I could and dived into the trunk of the tree, and tried to keep my beating heart silent. Could he hear it? I peeked again. He was gone.

Swoop! Snag! Bangrumble! The next thing I knew I was upside down. The goblin had swooped down from behind me and bundled me into a bag.

The bag was horrid and coarse. It scratched and rustled uncomfortably around me, and it smelt of fish. No doubt those fish had been carried to the goblin's cave and cooked. Would I be eaten too? I had plenty of time to worry about it.

The bag lurched this way and that as the goblin scurried and scramboodled up and down those white frozen hills. Oh why had I used the last of my Elf Dust on that stool? I could have used it now to turn the bag to mist and fall right through it and secretly run away. I was lying there all scrunched up and bouncing about when suddenly the bag opened and a clawed hand scooped me out. We had reached his hidden lair, a deep cave winding its way into the belly of a mountain. There was a fire burning, and the goblin hung me high over the dancing flames to slowly roast. Scratched across the wall of stone were the words: "GobDrop's Lounge." So this *was* the lair of the dreaded Christmas Goblin.

Well, *now* I was ever so sorry for wandering away from Santa's Lodge. I should have listened to the grown ups. Suddenly I didn't mind being Santa's Smallest Elf. I just wanted to be back with all the other elves. Hanging high over GobDrop's fire in a wide stone fireplace, I smelt the smoke and felt the heat from the licking flames.

I was hanging there, feeling miserable, looking all around me, when suddenly my eyes opened wide with surprise. There was someone else in the room. Someone very quiet, who sat very still staring up at me. It was a brilliant white Arctic hare.

I wanted to whisper over to him for help, but did not dare speak. Did the goblin know the hare was here? I barely had time to blink before the creature hopped away into the shadows and was gone.

Swinging there, thinking I was about to be cooked, I did not want to look into that fire. I kept staring into the shadows instead, hoping the eyes of that hare might reappear. What was the poor animal doing here? What hare would want to live with a goblin? Was the hare a prisoner, like me? Or was it perhaps trying to recover The Naughty List? Or rescue me?

I kept looking into the shadows, or up at the roof where the light and shade of the fire danced together in wavering patterns. The eyes did not reappear.

The fire began to sing with a slow crackle snappling sound. I did not want to think of those flames. Too soon I might be cooking inside them. But the more I wanted to look away, the harder it was. And when I stared at it, I saw the strangest logs burning there. They were tightly rolled from many leaves, and the leaves were of different colours, and they had pictures of human faces on them and human buildings.

And over that unearthly fire, so far from anything familiar, there in a cold cave in a white mountain hanging in a fish-smelling bag under the hard stare of a goblin, I forgot my courage and I began to cry.

Chapter Four
Do You Taste Nice?

GobDrop's wide eyes blinked and his long nose twitched. His grey tongue lashed along his fangs. Then suddenly he spoke in rhyme.

"Flames, flames, leap and stir,
out of the woods, forest and bur.
Lost all alone in the icy mountains
little elf cries like flowing fountains.
Small you are, but how do you taste?
Soon we'll see. Cook in haste!"

GobDrop licked his long purple lips again. I begged. I pleaded. I promised I would do anything I ever could to help him. The big goblin just looked at me and laughed:

"You help me,
little flea?
I am so big,
You are so small.
You can't help me,
I stand so tall."

I pleaded and promised to help GobDrop do all his chores. To gather water for his pot. To fetch wood for his fire. If only he promised not to eat me up. And to my surprise, he agreed. He hated housework more than almost any other thing except Christmas. But he disliked living in a mess.

And so that is how I came to be living in a cave, high up in the mountains, hidden from anywhere and everywhere else, with a goblin. Not just any goblin either, but GobDrop the Christmas Goblin. Think of it. Here I was living with him – and me, well, an elf from Santa's Lodge. And the smallest. I wished, in that moment, staring up into GobDrop's squinting eyes, that The Tallest Elf Of Them All would appear. He would show that goblin a thing or two.

But of course The Tallest Elf Of Them All was not here. It was just me and GobDrop, and the hidden Arctic hare, far from all other eyes to see. If you were ever inside GobDrop's cave you might understand how no elf had ever discovered it before me. The entrance to it was a long thin crack, big enough for a large human to crawl into. But the mouth of the lair lay undiscovered because it was wedged on all sides by tight lips of stone. Long ago it had become covered in thick ice that hung across the entrance like the folds of a frozen flower. Seen from afar it was just a patch of dazzling white hidden in a white landscape.

Inside, the cave was a long and winding tunnel of cool dark stone, that twisted its way up and down and roundabout. It was as though this place had once been forged by some giant burrowing worm.

It was my job to mop up the old layers of dust that had not been touched for tens or even hundreds of years, all along the entire length of the awkwardly winding tunnel. I would sweep, fetch wood, gather water, and GobDrop would hunt and bring back food, and cook it over his fire, and share it with me. Maybe he was not all bad, after all?

He would also ask me, sometimes, to tell him stories of Santa's Lodge. This was harder than gathering water or sweeping because it made me think of home. Talking about it made me want to weep for loneliness.

The goblin always seemed interested to know who had been promoted and who was in charge of what, especially anything to do with The Naughty List.

The Naughty List is one of Santa's top priorities. Father Christmas wants to make sure good girls and boys get the best presents. That's only fair, right? And elves are out there every week, every day, every moment, even now, watching and taking notes for The Naughty List. Are they watching you, right now? Look around and try to see a flicker in the corner of your eye where the colours you can see meet the ones you can't. That's where elves hide. Can you see anyone watching you?

The Naughty List is always updated. GobDrop seemed less interested in the updates, which I knew very little about anyway, and more interested in which elves were running it, of which I knew even less.

The Naughty List was one of Santa's most important documents, second in importance perhaps only to Santa's Book Of Rules, which told us what behaviour was expected from the elves in Santa's Lodge, and the things we could do – like ice flying – and the things we couldn't – like let in cats. There was not much to tell GobDrop, for I knew so little, but what I knew I told him. I did. I was worried about being eaten, and felt I had better do as I was told. How much would you have told him?

Then one day whilst I was busy cleaning, I suddenly came to a split in the tunnel. One path had a sign at the very place where the tunnel branched into two, scratched into a piece of old timber that stood on a pole made of old skulls.

The sign itself seemed to have been clawed, rather than painted or chiselled. Yes, clawed! And we all know whose claws it might have been who etched it, don't we? GobDrop, who had the sharpest, longest, meanest claws of all creatures living not just in that cave, but in the whole North Pole. And if the very depth of those scratches into that sign did not make the warning clear enough, the words themselves certainly did.

"Keep Out! Go No Further. Or you shall be swallowed by the ShuffleBelch. By Order of GobDrop The Goblin, King Under The Snows."

Chapter Five
The Lake Of The GarbleWarbles

I gasped. A ShuffleBelch? I thought they only existed in legends. In fact we elves will often use the term: "What ShuffleBelch!" when we find something very unlikely or completely ridiculous.

Stories about them say ShuffleBelch's are very basic creatures, worms, but about one hundred of your human metres long, and ten feet high. They are blind for they have no eyes, and deaf for they have no ears. They feel everything as vibrations, and in that way can hunt anything that moves. Their teeth jut out like stalactites from a mouth as round as a full moon.

Many an elf, I have been told, had last been seen as two legs kicking from that mawling, munching worm-mouth, all abristle with fangs.

So my earlier impression had been right. This whole tunnel had been chewed out by a gigantic worm gnawing slowly into the rock. And according to that sign it was still alive, somewhere in here. Was it somewhere near?

The sign said not to go up that path or I would be swallowed by the ShuffleBelch. Would you be careful and obey a sign like that? Or would you be a little daring and carry on to see what lay ahead?

Just as I was pondering what to do, and how serious the sign might be, I heard something huffing and chuffing and charumbling like a snoring dragon, just round the next bend. I stood there quivering and staring at the sign, mop in hand, wondering. Did I dare feed my nervous curiosity and carry on past the sign?

I didn't, not then. But instead I went down the other way, and found a huge underground lake. There on the damp drip, drip, dripping wall of the cave GobDrop had clawed the words:

"14,569 GarbleWarbles Live Here. And Counting."

I could see where other numbers, smaller ones, like 5, then 8, then 143, then further along, 3,567, then 6,760, and so on, had been scratched out, all across that corner of the cave wall.

What were GarbleWarbles, and were there really thousands of them in the lake beside me? I held my breath and stood very still, a sort of stillness humans just can't imagine, let alone imitate. My lungs did not move, my fingers were still as statues, even the follicles of my elven hair were rigid as if I was frozen in time. But time is a human illusion. Tick-tock, click-clock. We elves don't believe in time. But we do believe in change. And in that moment of frozen change, not a hair on my head dared quiver. By being so still, and changing colour to camouflage into the background hues which humans and many others creatures cannot see, we elves can make ourselves invisible.

Standing still and quiet in the shadows, I soon heard a splashing sound and little ripples began travelling across the top of the smooth water toward me. What was making them? Could it be one of the GarbleWarbles, or perhaps the giant worm?

Then I noticed some strange flying creatures leaping in and out of the water. I watched them breathlessly. They were very small. Much smaller than me, Santa's Smallest Elf. One could sit in my hand. They were covered in some strange mixture between feathers and fur, and seemed to flash little lights from their eyes each time they blinked.

I realised they were not so much leaping

in and out of the water, but bouncing across it. They called to each other with soft little garbling and warbling trills like the ringing of a bell smothered by cushions of cloud.

I could not help but smile, and with that upward crease of my lips and deepening of my cheeks, my elven invisibility was broken.

All of a sudden, with a terrific sploooosh of hundreds of tiny creatures diving all at once, the lake shimmered as they all leapt underneath the surface. Then there was silence, as the lake rippled this way and that, before hundreds of sets of tiny eyes appeared just above the surface, all staring at me. Each time they blinked, little lights of every colour shone for a moment then were gone.

So these were the GarbleWarbles. I could tell by their sound. I shivered as I thought of all the creatures that lived down here, in the hollow depths below the mountains, in GobDrop's winding cave. Bats, rats, UmberScats. Creatures known and unknown to humans. But none I felt sure were so fearsome as GobDrop himself, who had long ago declared himself the King Under The Snows.

His name made me gulp. I was his prisoner. He needed no locked door or chains to imprison me. The endless miles of snowy mountains meant I had no idea how to get home. I was in his cave, with nowhere else to go. I gathered my courage and bucket in hand, I walked toward the lake's edge. I watched the surface of that water very closely. I walked nearer, step by step. Would anything else pounce out at me?

I dipped in my bucket to get some fresh water. Splish! Splooosh! Some of it splashed on me. I jumped back. It was freezing.

It was then I noticed something. Leaves had been washed up on the shoreline, strange leaves like the ones GobDrop burnt in his fire.

They came in many colours, and sizes, but all had weird symbols scrolled across them, and pictures of human faces, or human buildings or machines, drawn onto their sides. Whatever could they be, and what were they doing here?

I bent to pick one up, and that's when I noticed many of them were half eaten, or less or more. Just as I saw that, one of the tiny creatures took courage and leapt out of the water, came skimming across it, and grabbed the strange papery leaf right out of my hand. It swallowed it, before blinking at me with a bright flash of its eyes and diving back into the water. I laughed. These little GarbleWarbles were just so cute.

I filled my bucket with clean water, and was just about to walk back up the tunnel when suddenly I heard a sound so loud the very roof trembled. Was it an ogre or the enormous ShuffleBelch worm?

The sound was coming from right above us and, to my horror, I saw out of the darkness that a great wave of leaves was rolling down from a hole in the roof, I had not noticed before. These strangely painted leaves fell down in a giant wave. As they fell through the air, the tiny creatures of the lake leapt across the water's surface and caught as many of the leaves as they could in their mouths. Then they gulped them down.

The whole hall was bright with the light of thousands of blinking eyes, flashing every colour against the cave walls. Only now did I see just how vast and immense a cavern this was.

The lake stretched away further than I could see, and everywhere these creatures were leaping and bouncing across the splashing surface of the water, munching in a frenzy on the unearthly leaves.

This lasted some moments and I stood there still and silent, wide eyed and mouth agape at the wonder of the marvellous sight before me. At last the storm of falling leaves came to a gradual end, with just a last few fluttering down like feathers caught in a breeze. The final few got caught in a draft of air and ended up by my feet. All was still. The tiny creatures had gone.

I scooped up my bucket and walked all the way back along that twisting pathway till I got to the place where I was mopping, and carried on with my work.

I was miserable. Why oh why had I been so foolish to ignore the warnings of my parents and the bigger elves, and wandered out alone?

However, even then I noticed that not everything they had said about GobDrop was absolutely true. I mean, for one thing, he did not have horns. And he might be miserable and mean, but he had let me stay in his cave and fed me well, albeit on dreadful goblin food.

Would you want to eat the legs of centipedes wrapped in butterfly wings? Or the whiskers of walruses? Me neither!

Chapter Six
A Lost List And A Missing Bag

I had been right about one thing. Back at Santa's Lodge nobody was missing me.

As the Christmas songs arrived, Santa practised each one keenly. Sometimes he practised them quietly in front of his fire, at other times he wandered outdoors and sang them to the reindeer, the snow wolves, the polar bears, the walruses or the seals.

And of course Santa sang each song to his elves, who loved to sit around and drift into the magical world of Santa's deep cherry and mistletoe voice.

Amidst building toys and gathering songs and applauding Santa's wonderful singing, nobody seemed to have time to notice that the smallest of all the elves had disappeared. Instead everyone agreed what a great mixture of songs they had gathered from across the world far and wide. There were old favourites sung a million times through many a year, others never heard before except in tiny hidden corners of the world and new songs by famous musicians still in the charts today.

And there amongst them all was the song especially written for Crystal, the little girl who gave him the idea in the first place. The thought of all good little boys and girls always makes Santa smile. This year he had a special smile just for Crystal, imagining her joy as she came downstairs on Christmas morning, to find Santa sitting under her Christmas tree, singing a special song just for her. Just like she asked for in her letter...

As Santa finished each song, he placed it in the bag of Christmas songs, knowing the magical bag would keep each song in perfect tune till he pulled it out. Finally, after weeks and weeks of gathering and learning, all the Christmas songs ever sung were in the bag, and Santa was ready.

Santa could hardly wait to leap into his sleigh, guide his flying reindeer to a Christmas market somewhere, and start singing. How happy the songs would make the adults and children out there in the world, just as people were seeming so sad and worried about not having enough money for presents. Where had all the money gone? Anyway, no matter.

Santa would show those humans. Joy was not about money. It was about giving and sharing, family and friends, and what better way to bring everyone together than a feast of Christmas songs. All the elves rubbed their hands together in glee. The songs would surely lift everyone's spirits.

There were still 21 nights until Christmas Eve when Santa's elves filled his sleigh with all those goodies people need to help prepare for the Christmas festivities: branches of holly for decoration, mistletoe for kissing under, new and exciting recipes for Christmas puddings.

And of course this year there was that extra something in Santa's sleigh: the bag of Christmas songs. It jingeringled and it jangerangled there in the back of The Sleigh surrounded by bands of red ribbon, spools filled with golden thread, and bright tinsel berries ready for hanging.

That evening, as the first soft light of the silver stars edged their gentle light into the sky, Santa was ready to fly. The breath of Santa's reindeer rose in warm mist into the Arctic air. They stood in pairs harnessed in rows, pawing at the cold ground with their sturdy hooves, their antlers waving at the sky.

Father Christmas leapt into the sleigh and

whistled to his reindeer, giving the reins a tug with one warm gloved hand.

"Up Comet, up Cupid, up Donner, up Blitzen. Go Dasher, go Dancer, go Prancer, and Vixen. With a hey and a ho and a dance and a berry, it's time to fly, let's make the world merry."

And quicker than the wind can catch a leaf, they were up and away speeding happily in the direction of your human cottages, towns, and cities.

Well that morning GobDrop tied some Goblin String around me and took me for a walk, just a single lash of it like a lead for a dog. Goblin String is not as strong as Elven Thread, but it can drag whole boulders up a mountain if a goblin is strong enough to pull it.

We climbed a steep and pointed snowy crag. GobDrop was carrying his old fish sack again. He lifted his head high into the air and that long nose of his wriggled. He was sniffing something out. GobDrop suddenly pulled something out from his pocket. It was a scroll of parchment, with the words The Naughty List scrawled across it in a careful elven hand.

I stopped in my tracks, and just pointed at the list, mouth open. GobDrop had The Naughty List right here in his claws.

What did he intend to do? Bury The Naughty List? Or throw me off the edge of his mountain? Or both? Maybe he would bury me and throw away the bag?

Then all of a sudden, out of nowhere, came the white hare, bounding down a large bank of glittering snow.

The goblin smiled and said:

"Here you go, little hare
see if you can make this fair.
Hop along and find a way
to help the List stick and stay.
The Naughty List
is such a farce,
everywhere
below the stars.
Not worth the paper it's written on,
no better than a Christmas song.
Good or bad,
right or wrong,
it makes no difference
where you belong.
But I shall not give up the fight
To help and switch wrong to... "

At that moment the lilting whisperings of

the bag of Christmas songs came toward us on the wind. The sound of those merry tunes made his eyes roll and his claws click. He squinted his eyelids as tight as he could and stared up into the sky. His nose twitched and his ears wiggled.

Way off in the distance, the tiny dot that was Santa's Sleigh was weaving across the sky. GobDrop realised it was going to be flying right above him in just a few minutes.

The goblin stuck his long claws in his pointed ears and shook his wrinkled head. He gnashed his teeth and stamped his feet and let out a terrible roar that rang across the valley.

The sound of that roar filled me with a chill so severe that I could not move. GobDrop danced those two spidery legs of his upon the steep icy rock and rattled his arms at the sky. And as he danced, as he shook, and as he wailed, the air all around him gathered into a dark cloud of meddlesome Goblin Storm.

GobDrop's claws pulled and prodded the storm into a ball of rain, that hung buffeting and billowing between his paws. The rain gathered into sleet, and the sleet turned into hail. GobDrop caught a great ball of hail in his arms, and threw it across the valley, straight into the belly of Santa's Sleigh.

Well you can imagine what happened next. One minute Santa was in his sleigh, leaning back in cruise mode as he sang and skimmed across the blue sky – and the next minute he was sitting in the middle of the wildest hailstorm the North Pole had ever seen. He grabbed the reins and pulled back a little to slow the reindeer down. Suddenly a ferocious fist of maddening fury seized The Sleigh and tipped it upside down. Santa gave a warning call to each of the reindeer.

"Blaze Comet, love Cupid, smash Donner, thunder Blitzen, charge Dasher, leap Prancer, spin Dancer, twirl Vixen. My fleet footed steeds hear my call, let's surf this mess, I have faith in you all."

With their antlers pointing down through the sky toward the mountain peaks below, and their hooves dancing upward below the stars, the reindeer flew on, eyes wide, ears back, following the tunnels between the wind.

These were not any old reindeer. These were Santa's reindeer. The reindeer the human who became Santa tamed, in those long ago days when he started building Santa's Lodge. These were the reindeer he had stabled and kept as his own and who had been allowed to drink from Santa's Cup on the night he found

The Magic. They were not to be pulled from the sky so easily.

With a gasp and a wink Santa and his troupe of flying friends pulled The Sleigh the right way up again. He steered half blind through the beating wall of ice. Then suddenly everything stopped: the roaring wind, the stinging hail, and the storm all seemed to pass just as quickly as it had begun. Santa beamed a smile at the sun as it blazed once more in the frozen blue sky, and laughed: "Wow, what a ride."

They flew on with a whistle. Santa slackened the reins, allowing The Sleigh to glide into cruise mode again. He stared back over his shoulder and saw such a mess in The Sleigh. The hawthorn and the mistletoe were all jumbled together. Broken tinsel berries lay amongst reams of torn red ribbon. Santa frowned. Then he groaned. The bag of Christmas songs was gone.

He slowed The Sleigh and began to fly lower and lower, in circles. Skimming over the white tops of the mountain peaks, Santa and his reindeer peered with alert eyes for any glimmer of the bag hidden somewhere among the snow. But there was no sign of it anywhere.

GobDrop lay crouched behind a large

white rock, licking his lips and grinning as he spied Santa's sleigh coming lower and lower into the valley. He watched as The Sleigh landed and Santa climbed out. He saw Santa walk this way and that, searching the snow but finding nothing.

GobDrop knew exactly where the bag of Christmas songs was. When the bag had fallen out he had used his Goblin Storm to catch it in mid air. As Santa blindly fought the storm, GobDrop wrapped the bag up in a fist of invisible mist and buried it deep in a pile of snow. GobDrop grinned and flicked his claws. The bag was there, right under Santa's boots, but it was deep under the snow and it was cloaked by a fist of Goblin Mist. GobDrop's fangs curved into a long and bristling grin: "It's just below your boots, you know. Can't you see? Ho Ho Ho!"

GobDrop sniggered quietly. He had to wrap his clawed hands about his gaping mouth, to stop Father Christmas hearing his giggles. Without help, Santa had no way of finding the bag in that endless landscape of shimmering white. It was buried under the snow, and it had also been turned invisibile by Goblin magic.

Chapter Seven
Finders Keepers

Would you have tried to help Santa find the bag? I wanted to. Believe me, I tried. But there was something in that scream the goblin had howled across the valley. There was a terrible loneliness and an aching anger. I felt it and the sadness of it froze me stiff.

I tried to call to Father Christmas, but my mouth and tongue were stuck. I tried to run but my legs ignored me. I stood there stiff and still. I tried to move a finger. Nothing. A thumb? Nothing still. I could move my eyeballs. Just!

So I watched helplessly as down in the valley Santa searched this way and that. Finally with a tremendous sigh and a tear in his eye he climbed back in his sleigh and flew off.

GobDrop waited till The Sleigh and Santa's reindeer were well out of sight then he clambered down from his high perch. On those long wiry legs of his he bounced down the craggy peaks. And to my delight as he leapt away, the line of Goblin String that was binding me like a dog lead, finally came loose. It was just lying there in the snow. Happiness sparked in my heart again, just for a moment, and that was all I needed. I was free. I could run away while GobDrop went for the bag. Or... or I could try to get to the bag before him, and snatch it right out from under his claws.

I have learned a few things from older elves. Like a bad thing is made even worse when a good elf does nothing to help.

GobDrop was ahead of me, and he was fast. He cartwheeled across the snow to where the bag of Christmas songs lay hidden. Then he stopped on the frozen patch right above where it lay buried. I was still sliding down a snowy slope as he began to dig those long claws of his into the frosty floor.

He belched and burped happily as he dug the bag up, and with a click of his claws, he released it from the ice. The sheen of the sharpness on those claws made me hold back a scream. I went kamrundering down the slope, somersaulted straight between the goblin's paws and grabbed the bag on my way through.

The startled look on GobDrop's face would have made me laugh if I had been a little further from those claws. I took one glimpse as I tumbled past him and then I hit the ground running. I had the bag of Christmas songs in my hands. Everyone would notice me now.

All I had to do was outrun this goblin, find my way home across the unknown mountains and ring on the door to Santa's Lodge. What a surprise those bigger elves would get. This would start them talking. And nobody would ignore me, or call me too small, not ever again.

Remember that I told you how fast we elves are out on the snow. I have snow slid all my life. And I am pretty good at it. And right then, at that moment, my feet moved like they have never moved before.

I was woobangering along at a brilliant speed, feeling the rush of the wind. I glanced behind me, with that bag of Christmas songs in my little hand, and could see GobDrop right behind me, limlumbering happily along.

He was almost smiling, looking as if he was enjoying this chase. He was in his element. But I would show him.

I was just putting on another burst of speed, when out of the white snow popped a white head with long white ears and two bright eyes. It was the hare, the Arctic hare I had seen in GobDrop's cave that day when I first arrived. The hare he had been just about to hand The Naughty List to. And he bounded along right under my feet, and I tripped. I fell. The bag fell too, but I did not let it go.

GobDrop's grinning, fanged face and twitching nose appeared over me, and before I could even gasp, he had scooped me and the bag of Christmas songs up and thrown us both inside his old sack. And yes, it still smelt of old fish.

I shimbrungled about in that sack as we journeyed across valleys, over mountains, and through winding trails until we reached GobDrop's cave.

As soon as we entered he dumped me out of the bag and gave me a large wooden spoon. He wanted me to warm yesterday's dinner — eagle eyes and fish bone stew.

The flames laughed and spat as they ate into the tightly rolled, papery logs.

GobDrop could hardly wait to rip open the bag of Christmas songs and empty it into the flames of his fire. But first, he wanted to gloat for a moment.

He danced around in glee with the bag in his hands, listening to the songs crash and barumble and kerfundle around inside.

Now I knew about the sadness in the world outside, all the elves did, and of that little girl Crystal's letter, and how Santa had sent elves out to every part of the globe to find the songs. I, SnowShine, Santa's Smallest Elf had to do *something* to stop the goblin from burning those songs.

I watched GobDrop leaping and lurching about in glee as he jiggled the bag and muttered:

"Fire, fire, jumping flame,
things will never be the same!
Notes burn,
money gone,
now take a turn,
with Christmas songs..."

Did I hear that right? Were those strange papery logs really wads of human money he was burning? And was he feeding it to the GarbleWarbles too? It was the same stuff in his fire and in the lake. What was he up to?

Then to my horror he used those hairy springy legs of his to leap into the fire. With his thick eyebrows all a twitch, he raised the bag above his head. One second more and the songs would be sizzling in the flames.

I jumped up and held my tiny hands as high as I could, which was not very high at all.

"Stop, stop!" I cried.

GobDrop turned on me and gave me a mean look.

"What did you say, little SnowSlime?"

(I don't think he *meant* to make my name nasty, it's just the goblin way, goblins find nasty things much easier to remember.)

I stood up as brave and tall as I could, which was not very tall, as you know, and not the very least bit brave. But *I* was all I had. I had to think of something nasty fast – something GobDrop would like the sound of, something that would save the songs. If I failed then the world would be without Christmas songs forever. At first I stammered, "Uh, uh uh..."

GobDrop echoed me. "Uh, uh, uh!" he taunted, tilting his heavy head mockingly this way and that.

"Oh GobDrop." I said. "I am just SnowShine. Santa's Smallest Elf. There is nothing I can do to stop you. But I think you might want to stop yourself. If you burn those songs all in one go, what a waste of the nasty fun you could have. You are the most feared goblin of them all. Why not stretch out the meanness a little, you know, just let the songs sweat uncomfortably a little first?"

To my amazement GobDrop actually listened to me. The thought of those songs sizzling in discomfit, sweating in the bag over the rising heat of his fireplace, made him grin so wide his furry, unbrushed razor teeth gleamed their brightest yellow. He took the bag and hung it from a nasty hook above his fire.

GobDrop's Cave

Chapter Eight
Save Our Songs

Well I sat in that cave staring up at the bag for hours, marvelling at the way it seemed to twinkle and shine. I waited until GobDrop fell asleep, then crept to the fireside. That hook hung very high. Could I reach it? I prepared for an elf jump straight up, one, two, three... and I sprung as high as I could.

Well, I missed the bag on my way up but caught it on the way down. I held my ear to the bag and heard a soft tinkling murmur inside. I put my long elf fingers into the strap that held the bag shut at the top, and wiggled it this way and that until it loosened. Then I started to open the bag – just a tiny bit. Ah the music that came out! It made a merry leap and echoed loudly through the cave.

"Jingle bells, jingle bells..."

"Shhhhhhhhh!" I whispered urgently to the bag. What if the goblin woke up? The bag was woven with elven magic and it heard me and obeyed, becoming much quieter. Its soft song swelled my heart with happiness and longing. But still I was terrified that GobDrop would wake up. Soon, I forced myself to shut the bag tight.

This happened each night. As GobDrop's eyes closed and his breathing became a goblin snore, I opened the bag of Christmas songs just a little, to hear those delicious carols. There in that cold cave I felt the beauty of Christmas just by listening to them.

GobDrop always told me that the outside world was full of wickedness and greed — even amongst all the Christmas cheer. But I knew that wasn't true. I also knew it was only a matter of time till the goblin got bored with watching the songs hanging there over the fire.

The dancing flames ate on and on into the endless piles of paper logs made from tightly rolled human money. Soon enough GobDrop would throw the songs in there, I was sure.

Back at Santa's Lodge everyone had been thrown into a panic and sorrow at the loss of the bag of Christmas songs. Of course nobody had been thrown into panic or sorrow over the loss of me! They still hadn't even noticed that I'd gone missing. They would only miss me when a tangle occurred in the Elven Thread which was so bad that nobody else could fix it. Then they would discover that I was gone and then they might come looking. But for now Santa and his elves fought desperately against time to make sure that their surprise had not backfired terribly. They were frantic. What if, thanks to them, this was the first Christmas without songs?

While the elves searched far and wide for the bag of Christmas songs, Santa began writing and practising some brand new ones – just in case...

Santa was very sad, and this made writing the songs a very difficult task indeed. But Santa found inspiration from the kindness of the elves, the roar of his fire, the mountain of toys waiting to be delivered to girls and boys, and the memories of Christmas past. He is Santa after all and he must set a good example but sometimes being everyone's role model must be a heavy burden.

While Santa sat writing new songs, his elves frantically searched the snowy slopes to find the bag. That is how, one cold and frosty morning, I happened to be sat at the mouth of GobDrop's cave, staring out at my prison when I saw a tiny glimmer of colour high up on a slope. I watched intently, my eyes wide with hope and surprise. I watched the way that light sparkled and moved easily over the ice and across the slopes. There was only one creature I could think of that had a sparkle like that and moved so gracefully on treacherous ground. It had to be one of Santa's elves. My heart leapt.

I, SnowShine, Santa's Smallest Elf, had to think fast. It would have been dangerous enough if GobDrop was asleep, but this was early and as usual the goblin was out there in the snow somewhere, hunting. Had he seen the elf coming toward us? If he had, he would try to catch it for his breakfast. I had to warn the elf, and tell him I had the bag of Christmas songs.

Would you have run out to try to warn the elf?

I ran from that cave as quickly as I could. My heart was beating so loudly I wondered if the goblin might hear it. I ran up that icy mountainside as only an elf can. Nervously peering this way and that for GobDrop, I climbed higher and higher, getting ever closer to the elven glimmer, which was coming gradually toward me. With one last skip over a craggy finger of ice I reached the elf.

She was beautiful and her eyes shone with surprise and kindness as she looked down upon me from under a silver cloak. With a cloak like that she might well be invisible to all but other elves like me. Perhaps GobDrop could not see her after all?

Elven cloaks are a great delight for my folk, for we love the element of surprise. But it was she, and not I, who got the surprise as I leapt onto the path in front of her.

I told the big elf that I had wandered off, wanting to be The Tallest Elf Of Them All by looking down from the highest mountain top, but had become lost. I said I was being kept as a servant by GobDrop the Christmas Goblin, doing his cooking and washing his dishes and mopping his floors.

The elf's silvery eyebrows raised in wonder as I told her all this, but they went higher still when I explained that the bag of Christmas songs was hanging over GobDrop's fire. I warned her that GobDrop wanted to burn the songs and she had better disappear fast and come back with help. I warned her that the elves must be very careful because GobDrop is larger than them and very strong.

Well, the big elf wanted to take me with her straight away so I was safe. I could have gone with her there and then, but what about the bag? I told her I was safe, and it was the bag that would be in peril if GobDrop saw that I had gone. This was not *exactly* true for I knew I could be in big trouble if GobDrop had seen me talking to the other elf

Would you have gone back with the elf? Back to Santa's Lodge where now everyone would notice you for helping to find the bag, wanting to hear all your stories about living with the dreaded Christmas Goblin? Or would you have gone alone, back to that cold cave to try to keep the bag of Christmas songs safe?

When I got back to the cave, all was silent. I began to brush GobDrop's floor, hoping that the elf would get back before too long with some helpers.

The goblin was out in the woods hunting with the snow-white hare bounding along beside him when he heard Santa coming. Santa was singing a Christmas song at the top of his voice as he flew The Sleigh over the mountain peaks and down toward us. It was a song about saving the bag of Christmas songs. This was Santa Magic!

GobDrop jumped around on his long legs and waved his fists. He began to dance and prance and grimrumble, gathering Goblin Storm in his claws.

But this time he was too late. Santa was too close. When he saw Santa flying straight towards him, the goblin screeched and ran for his cave. But I knew the goblin was not running away from Santa. He was running to get the bag of Christmas songs before Santa could stop him.

I was at the cave entrance watching the chase and believe me it was a close thing, who was going to reach the cave first? GobDrop, on his own, was probably the fastest runner in the North Pole. But Santa was not alone. He had his eight reindeer pulling him along. Santa's sleigh was faster but further away. Gobdrop was moving as quickly as he could. He was nearly at the cave's mouth, with Santa hot on his heels.

I held my breath hoping Father Christmas would reach me first, but it was not to be. GobDrop hurtled into the cave with his tongue drooling and his claws clicking and his eyes wide with panic. I, Snowshine, Santa's Smallest Elf, stretched out my arms to try to stop him, but he grabbed the bag from over my head and threw it into the fire. He did not want a world full of Christmas songs, and he hoped to destroy them all. I gasped, there was nothing more I could do. The first Christmas without songs was upon us.

I thought the bag would burst into flames. But this was of course a very magical bag, made by elven hands, and the sound of Santa singing 'Saving the bag of Christmas songs' added to its protection. The fire of human money could not burn it. The songs were safe, as long as the bag stayed shut.

GobDrop pulled the bag out of the fire and dug his claws into it, tearing its elven fibres this way and that, as the bag whistled and jingled. Then came the ring of the reindeers' harness just outside the cave mouth and Santa stood there in the doorway. All the reindeer were there too, antlers held at the ready like piercing knives. GobDrop's eyes opened wide with fright and in a quavering voice he called:

"Help!"

Now that did surprise me. Would you have helped the goblin? I didn't.

Less than a moment later, he jumped past Santa's boots and ran off with a shriek. That puzzled me too. I didn't think he was such a coward. I guess he did not want to get told off and punished by Santa. GobDrop is huge and powerful, but everyone knows his magic is no match for Father Christmas.

Santa came into the cave and his face was

beaming. He picked the bag out of the fire and with a generous 'Ho. Ho. Ho!" he climbed back into his sleigh. It was full of ribbons and fruits, parcels, nuts and berries. I blushed as Santa sat me on his knee and called for the reindeer to take flight. Up we went into the sky.

Santa wasted no time. With the bag of Christmas songs in his sleigh he set off to complete the journey he began almost three weeks ago, travelling the world to sing Christmas songs and bring everyone some cheer. Only now he had some new songs, ones that Santa would never have written, if GobDrop had not interfered. And best of all, I, SnowShine, Santa's Smallest Elf, got to travel in The Sleigh and see all the world's wonders by his side.

Chapter Nine
A Magical Sleigh Ride

Well I don't know about human children, but we young elves are always wishing we can have a go in The Sleigh, and almost no one ever can. Santa keeps The Sleigh to himself because it has to carry so many presents and even a magical sleigh like this one can only carry so much. It just manages, when it is bulging almost to overbrimming, to hold enough presents for every child in the world. At least, enough for all of the good ones.

I did quietly wonder about that though, while I was up there in The Sleigh. Here I was, yet I had been naughty, hadn't I? Running off like that in the first place and getting lost. But I guess that something good came from my bad behaviour. If I had not been there then the bag of Christmas songs would have been lost forever. My naughtiness led to something good for others. That was the difference. That was why I was given such a great treat: to fly with Santa in his sleigh.

Up there it seemed as if the whole world was made of tall mountains covered in snow. That was all we saw as we flew on and on, over endless peaks.

I had to laugh at myself. When I'd set off from Santa's Lodge, I'd thought that if I climbed the mountain I could see from Santa's front door, it would put me on top of the world.

It sort of did, but as you know there was a higher mountain right next to it. There were lots of higher mountains. We were flying above them now. They looked like they ruled the world when seen from the ground, but from up here, they looked like tiny peaks of icing on a cake.

Suddenly, we were flying past them, over wide waters dotted with the glimmering shine of giant icebergs. My eyes opened wide in wonder. GobDrop's lake was the biggest expanse of water I had ever seen, but that was tiny compared to this open stretch of sea. It reached right out with its frozen fingers to stroke the gentle curve of the world.

But if the floating icebergs made my eyes wide with surprise, wait till I, SnowShine, Santa's Smallest Elf, caught site of the glimmering lights of my very first human city. It looked like a thousand fairy lights had all come on at once and were twinkling without end.

On Christmas morning, I was even allowed to watch through the window when Santa sang to Crystal, the girl who had asked for her very own Christmas song.

When we finally got home after one of the best Christmases ever, everyone celebrated. All the elves wanted to talk to me. Santa announced that I was to receive a special Santa Award.

The bigger elves all made a fuss of me. They brushed my hair, polished my boots and let me choose my very own crystal chair. Flags of shimmering starlight that sparkled my name were strung along the great halls and corridors. There were balloons with my face on them. The hum and lilt of minstrels practising songs about *me*, Santa's Smallest Elf, echoed down the halls.

When that special day came Santa lined everyone up – all the elves and seals and polar bears and wolves – and in front of them all, he gave me a Santa Award. It was a brand new badge to wear, saying 'Santa's Bravest Elf'.

Father Christmas smiled at me and said, "SnowShine, you are small on the outside, but tall as a mountain on the inside."

All I could do was smile the largest smile any elf had ever seen.

GobDrop's Story

Chapter One
Santa's Naughtiest Elf

A h yes. You all feel happy for little SnowSlime don't you? But you only know half the story. It's true that I was a bit of a bully. Calling him SnowSlime instead of SnowShine. Talking to him with nasty rhyming poems and making him scared and all.

But I want to win you over, so I'll start my side of the tale by being nice and using his proper name. Because something happened to me when I met SnowShine. Something that has made me decide to stop bullying forever. SnowShine is Santa's littlest elf, true enough. But what you may not know is that I was Santa's naughtiest elf. Yeah! Me! Your new friend GobDrop.

That's right. I was once an elf. I was Santa's naughtiest elf as I just said, and his biggest elf. I was, and I still am, The Tallest Elf Of Them All. So SnowSlime – sorry, I mean SnowShine – got his wish. He said he always wanted to meet the Tallest Elf didn't he? Well here I am! Now before little SnowShine was even born, I was helping to make toys at Santa's Lodge. I bet you did not expect to hear that, did you? There are always two sides to every tale.

I expect you have heard about me?

Probably from Santa's gossiping elves. SnowShine started off his story by moaning about how nobody knew anything about him and they all ignored him. Well everyone knows me all right, except they've got it wrong! What they've heard is not all true.

You see stories grow and stories spread. People talk about me, but they only say bad things. In a way, it would be better if nobody had ever heard of me, because what they've heard makes them think I am not worth knowing.

Why am I even bothering to tell you this story? Because as I see it, SnowShine left it unfinished. It was a happy ending but he missed something out at the very end. He left out something very important, and I reckon that he left it out on purpose.

So what was I saying? Oh yeah. I lived there, in Santa's Lodge. I liked it. I bet you would love to sit there all day surrounded by elves wouldn't you? Lots of elves and magic. And toys. Making the wishes of all the good girls and boys come true. But that's where my problems began. With The Naughty List – or with The Naughty Lists to be grammatically correct, as a fresh list arrived every day. I was put in charge of them. And at first everything that came in on those lists used to really shock me. But as I sat there reading how one boy did this, or some girl did that, and they needed to be struck off and stopped from getting the best toys – well, I started to notice that something was going wrong.

Out there in the world of humans, things were not always working the way that Santa wanted. Some kids who were being really good were getting very little, while others who were spoilt and selfish got too much.

Every evening I had to report to Santa. I went to him and told him the names of the naughty girls and boys – they were all on the List. It's up to Santa, and not me, to distribute the presents. He's the Big Man, as you know, a human who got himself a patch of earth at the North Pole and built it into a toy workshop. And while laying the foundation for that workshop he found some magic to help him become one of the most powerful human wizards of all time.

I trusted that guy with the red suit to make sure The Naughty List – which is after all *his*

Naughty List – was correct. But then Christmas came, and Christmas went, and those elves who worked for me, started to bring me disturbing news. The Naughty List was going wrong.

I was furious about what was happening. The bad kids were often getting bigger and better presents than the good kids. It was so unfair!

So I went to report to Santa. That's something only the bigger elves must do. I tried to tell Father Christmas it was unfair. I wanted to understand how it could happen. He just talked to me with that calm, kind voice of his and told me not to worry. I stayed quiet. Father Christmas is no fool. He likes to reward goodness because he says it makes the world a better place. But I was disappointed with Santa, because Santa simply wasn't doing anything about the problem.

Things got even worse when I discovered that Santa breaks his own rules. Even though he wrote them down in his Book Of Rules. Now don't get me wrong. Father Christmas is a nice guy. Or at least he tries to be. He wants to do what is right and best. But as I have said, he breaks his own rules. I can prove it.

Chapter Two
Santa Claus Has A Secret

Shall I tell you a secret? With this information I could really bring the Big Man down. I could if I wanted. Here it comes... Sssshhhhhh... but can you keep a secret? Ok. Santa has a cat. A big white fluffy one.

He puts long white ears on it so if you went peering in through his window, you might think it was an Arctic hare. Arctic hares are welcome in Santa's Lodge, according to Santa's Book Of Rules. This is because they pose no threat to elves. Cats pose a threat, a serious one, and are not allowed anywhere in the building. Santa obviously knows what trouble cats can cause in halls and underground tunnels full of elves.

We have stories and songs written about the brave elven warriors who fought off and defeated various cats through the history of Santa's Lodge. Cats are hunters, and will hunt anything that is smaller than them that happens to be seen hurrying along the ground. That means mice, rats, beetles, spiders, all sorts of creatures.... and busy Christmas elves. Cats hunt elves so Santa wrote a law saying Santa's Lodge was a feline-free zone. Cats are not allowed.

Cats don't scare me. I may not be Santa's Biggest Elf anymore, he stripped me of that title when he threw me out of the Lodge. I am not now 'Santa's *anything* Elf'. I am not *his* at all. I don't belong to Santa like some stuffed toy. I belong to me. And I may not be Santa's Biggest Elf, but I am still The Tallest Elf Of Them All. And I am not afraid of cats. They are afraid of me. And Santa, if you asked him, would probably say he keeps his cat cosy and warm in his own private apartments, where no elves ever go. So he gets to have a pet cat, like other humans do, and we elves are kept safe. But his apartment is in Santa's Lodge. And his cat is too. So Santa is still breaking a rule.

I found out about Santa's big, white, fluffy cat one evening when I was staring in through his window. I'd got something important to tell him so went to report to Santa but it was out of hours. I knocked. No answer. Maybe he was out.

So I peered in through the window and there was this white cat, with rabbit ears on, and at first I thought what an odd looking hare, when all of a sudden it leapt up onto the mantelpiece, and the ears fell right off. I could hardly believe my eyes. A cat! There in Santa's own apartment.

About the same time that I found out about Santa's cat, I discovered some more bad news. This time it was staggering. The humans were taking things into their own hands. Some bad kids were getting the coolest presents, while some good kids were getting precious little. And as more and more news reached my ears, I realised it all came down to one thing: money.

Chapter Three
A Few Things That I'll Never Understand

I don't understand money. No elves do. We work tirelessly for Santa, and we never get paid. And Santa, even though he is human, tells us he has no more idea of it than we do. He never touches the stuff.

Some human inventions are very cool. We love the round glittering globes of little mirrors all in a ball, created by a famous human artist called Andy Warhol who made it for a band called The Velvet Underground to hang over their stage. Then other humans made smaller versions to hang as decorations on their Christmas trees. So yes, we like some human inventions: water fountains, kites, hot-air balloons and bubble gum. But there are many human inventions that we elves, and Santa, do not deal with. Money is one of them.

That's right. Money is an invention. Did you ever even think of that? A human thought it up, and you must all like it, because you all use the stuff. But money is unfair. Some people have so much, others have so little. But as elves say, money is not important. It is fun, laughter, creativity, adventure and love that count. Even I, GobDrop the dreaded Christmas Goblin, know that.

I did not understand Santa. He wanted the best-behaved kids to get the best presents. That made perfect sense. But why waste a lot of time sending elves out all over the world, writing lists of who was good and who was not, but then not doing anything much with the information?

Santa tried to make sure that The Naughty List was obeyed. There was a whole enormous room for good kids where the best toys were made, things like rocking horses and tree houses, swimming pools and bouncy castles. And a little room for the smaller toys, things like yoyos and dice for the naughty kids. Everyone got something, good or naughty, but to get one of those big presents from that enormous room, you had to behave.

But the whole idea was being vandalised by humans and their money. Money meant that naughty kids with rich parents got bigger presents. And Santa wasn't doing anything about it. I was not supposed to meddle in human affairs. Someone had to do something! But what?

So I started to read the Naughty Lists, hunting for ideas. Unrolling the endless parchment, I read about all sorts of mischief. Some kids in England filled their teacher's lunch box with ants. That made me laugh. Some kid in Africa bullied smaller kids. Naughty. No toys for you. (That one got a big X next to their name).

This wasn't what I was looking for. I needed to find something exceptional, something genius – an idea that would help me take the money away from the humans and get the Naughty List working again.

At last I found it. There on the list was a note about a nasty big sister who was stealing her little sister's money from under the pillow after the Tooth Fairy came. It might just work!

Elves and fairies are not usually on talking terms. We have different magic and each kind sticks with their own. But I had heard that there were places in deep and ancient woods where fairies live below the roots of enormous trees, in long winding tunnels below the forest. Delicate light glows from the fairies' wings as they work.

Sometimes even humans who can only see 1 out every 1000 colours, can see the fairy light shine for a moment through a crack below the roots, but usually the fairies remain invisible to people. Nearly always.

In those same forests, so I have heard, live wood elves, in tall towering tree trunks that have become hollow. These elves make winding stairs and grand halls, and all sorts of rooms – rooms for eating, rooms for weaving, rooms for magic, rooms for talking, rooms for thinking and rooms for day dreaming – all there carved inside their hollowed out trees. In such places, I have heard, elves and fairies share the same forests, and they all live their lives in relative peace. They share the same turf, so I guess it makes sense to be good neighbours.

That girl who stole her little sister's money from the Tooth Fairy had given me an idea. I decided to go to those forests and get in touch with some fairies. The wicked ones. Not all fairies are good you know. Not all of *anything* is good. In fact, I was starting to think that maybe, GobDrop, Santa's Biggest Elf, was not so good either.

It was a long way to those forests, but I journeyed there. I went to find a naughty fairy, to ask him or her to follow the Tooth Fairy around, and steal back all the money left under sleeping children's pillows! It seemed like the perfect way to rid the world of money.

Well at first, things went pretty well. I found a mischievous forest fairy: The Naughty Toothless Fairy, as she came to be known. She liked my plan, and she did an excellent job of secretly following the Tooth Fairy around, and taking the money she left without waking up the sleeping children.

I was taking money out of the human world, but it was very, very slow. And it made a lot of children cry, which was not what I wanted.

We did that for a whole year, but the following Christmas, it seemed to make no difference at all. Some of the worst kids were still getting great presents bought for them.

I needed to get rid of more money. The Toothless Fairy did find a few houses where humans kept thousands and thousands of notes all rolled up tight under their mattresses, and sure enough when the human went to use it, it was gone. But that was a drop in the ocean.

So I started to wonder if humans had another place where they hid their cash, apart from under their beds? To take money away from humans, to set things right with The Naughty List, I had to think up something much bigger, much vaster than just The Toothless Fairy working alone. I had to take the money away on a far bigger scale. So I sent out my team of elves to find out where humans hid their mountains of money, not telling them why I needed to know.

That's the trick with being naughty. Not the trick you do, but the trick that happens *to* you. The one you did not plan. Sometimes you try to start out being naughty because, strangely, it seems the right thing to do in the circumstances. And maybe it is. But then you do another naughty thing to help or cover up the first one, then another to cover up that, and start telling little lies to hide it all. And bigger lies to hide them. And soon enough you have lost the truth, and have lost yourself, sure as in a deep dark wood at night, and suddenly you realise you have gone bad. It's not a nice feeling, believe me.

Rumours begin about you. They say I was trying to stop Christmas, but no! I was trying to stop money.

Chapter Four
My Money Binning Idea

Then one day, I was reading the latest Naughty List and I saw it. There was some kid in Canada who had used a magnet to suck up all his parents metal – knives, forks, spoons, clocks, car keys, and most interestingly, their coins. He hid it all in a drawer under his sister's bed. His parents could not find their missing stuff anywhere. They ended up having to eat with their fingers, and they turned up late for everything – because they had no clocks. Anyway, that's where I came by the idea. Could I make some sort of money magnet, that would suck up human money and hide it all away?

I walked straight down to report to Santa. I hoped this time he would come around to my way of thinking. To my dismay he did not go for it. Once again, he said it would be meddling in human affairs, and that interfering broke the law that was set down in Santa's Book of Rules.

Disappointed, I tried to forget all about it. But the more I heard, the more frustrated

I became. It appears that not only did some humans use money to buy naughty kids great presents, they were actually pretending these gifts were from Santa himself. Impostors! Cheats! You see, Santa is real. And so are elves. And fairies. But when an adult human pretends they are Santa, the kid might someday find out. That kid tells another one. And for the parent who pretended to be Santa, if they ever own up to their children, what a disaster!

When a human child stops believing in Santa, they stop believing in the rest of us too. Santa is a figurehead for all that is magical in the world of children. Take the real Santa away from the heart of a child and you take away everything else magical too. Imagine a world with no magic. It's a world where potions are soup and spells are empty riddles. I would not want to live in a world like that, where seeing is believing, and you forget there are some things that are real, that you will never see. You forget there are two sides to every story.

The more I thought about it, the more that it all seemed to point to money. I don't understand money. I never went to school or studied maths. For me: 1 + 2 + 3 = LOTS. But what I do understand is that some humans are very good at maths. They know the difference between 3, and 33, and 33,333,333,333. That's such a big number that I bet some grown up humans don't know what it is. But some people WANT IT ALL. They want it for themselves, and they want it now. It's all about money for them. Not kindness, or music, or stories or laughter. Not Love. Not even happiness itself. It's just about money. Money stops The Naughty List working. And people get confused and stop trusting Santa. And bad kids get big presents.

So I went to Santa for a final time and I pleaded with him. I begged. Please could we build a money magnetising machine? It would solve the problem. Let humans live just one year with no money, I said. Sure, at first they would panic, wondering how could they eat without it. But they don't eat money. They eat food. Not the sort of food that elves eat – swallowing mouthfuls of sunshine, gulping gusts of wind, sipping gentle moonlight. Humans eat a mix of what monkeys, hares, and wolves do – bananas, pears, lettuce, carrots, bacon, beef, that sort of thing. So they would not miss their money.

But Santa just shook his head and said that it was forbidden to meddle in human affairs, and that was that. But somehow that did not sound quite right, to me, coming from him. I mean, he meddled, right? By trying to give good kids better presents, and naughty kids not such good ones. That was meddling. Except, of course, the humans were meddling back and the rich kids were getting better presents.

So you know what? I decided to go ahead and build the money magnetising machine without Santa's permission.

Doing it in secret wasn't easy. All day every day I was there reading The Naughty List, with elves bustling and rustling and chiseling and hammering and painting all around me.

Building the machine was only possible in the changeover when the night shift began – yes there are shifts at Santa's Lodge, just like in human factories. As those who worked by day left, and those who worked by night came, in that great heave of elf bodies flitting this way and that, it was in those moments, and just before supper, that I started to build the machine that would save Christmas.

I sat there hammering and chiseling, beating and drilling, grabbing moments here and there when nobody was watching. Days became weeks and weeks became months. The machine got bigger and bigger: with funnels here and spouts there. It had tubes and wires and cylinders and a massive pump. At last, the day came when it was finally ready. There was a big green button with the word GO written on it. But before I pressed that button, I stopped.

When you invent something, you get to give it a name. What was I going to call my machine? The place where money is stored and kept secret and safe, I found out, was called a 'bank'. And the human who takes the money and keeps it locked away is called a 'banker'. I've often heard humans grumbling about these bankers, saying that they are always trying to take people's money and keep as much of it for themselves as they could. That's what my machine was designed to do: suck money from unsuspecting humans! So that's what I called my machine: The Banker.

I stuck out my long elegant elf finger to push that green GO button. But I stopped for a second time and I hesitated. Santa had told me not to do it - but I was sure it would bring good to the world and help The Naughty List do its job properly again.

My finger trembled.

Would you have pushed that big green GO button?

Chapter Five
Push The Button!

Once I pushed the button there was no going back. The machine howled like a disgruntled giant as cogs and pumps and dials and funnels whirred and weewongled into action.

That huge magnet made especially for money pulled notes and coins secretly and silently off the humans. It sucked the money from their pockets, from their piggy banks, from their wallets and purses, from underneath mattresses, below floorboards and behind picture frames. The Banker sucked it all in, slowly but surely.

When the elves secretly borrowed everyone's Christmas songs, they did their magic well before Christmas, before anyone was even thinking about Christmas carols, so nobody noticed they had gone. But the money – well, when that started to go missing, the humans noticed. And they panicked. The Banker wasn't a clever machine. It also took money from the poor humans as well as the rich. That is where my plan went kind of wrong. Except, it didn't! I wanted no money to be left anywhere in the world. If nobody had any, everyone would have to help each other without being paid. And The Naughty List would work again. As I say, this was not a loan – this was theft. I had no intentions of giving it back.

Each day between the day shift and night shift, I tended the machine. I added oil, and water, and sunshine.

And as that machine chuffled and buffled and bangalooed, puff bloomed and smoke smangoogled. I was there breathing it in, and weird things began to happen to me. My legs started to lengthen, my eyebrows started to bristle, my body began to grow a thick covering of green and purple fur, my teeth turned sharp and grew a fuzzy yellow slime. Long claws sprouted from my fingers and toes. Now I looked more like a goblin than an elf.

Even my appetite changed. Elven food was not enough. I started to head off into the wilderness to hunt. I began to wear long cloaks with deeper hoods and trailing sleeves, to hide the transformation that was happening to me.

Looking back, I was very foolish. I was bound to get caught sometime. This was not one of the elven inventions that work busily away without making a sound. Nope, once pumped into action, The Banker roared. As it got louder and louder I put an Elf Silence spell on it, and just to be sure added some Elf Dust to make it invisible. But with a machine that is twisting and turning and tumbling like this, spells can slip off. I had a machine that I could not hide forever.

And what was I to do with all the money? I did not want to burn the money, or slice it up into a zillion pieces. No! I hoped to do something useful with it. I just wasn't sure what. I did not mean to spend it. Oh no! Not at all! Why would an elf want to spend money? We have no need of the strange, troublesome human stuff.

Well there I was one evening, as elf workers scurried this way and that. I was busy sprinkling a fresh layer of Elf Dust, onto the machine when who walked in but Santa Claus himself! Five winks later I was outside Santa's Lodge in the snow. The Big Man had thrown me out. He said I had disobeyed him, and was not to be trusted anymore.

Everyone was there. Everyone was watching. All the elves who had looked up to me, admired me, respected me, they were all there peering at me, from the door and the windows and the rooftops.

In front of everyone, Santa said: "GobDrop, you've let me down. You have broken the law, which is clearly written in my Book of Rules. If you can't live honestly by my rules, you'll have to leave and live somewhere else. I'm afraid that you are no longer GobDrop, Santa's Biggest Elf.'

One of the cheekiest elves, who was nearby called out:

"That's right. Now he's GobDrop – the Christmas GOBLIN!!!"

Some of the other elves took up the chant – but Santa got cross and ordered them to be silent. The naughty elf's words were hard but there was some truth in them. For a goblin is an elf gone wrong, disobedient, and dishonest.

How do you think I felt with everyone watching, everyone listening, and Santa telling me to leave? His helpers were calling me a goblin, a twisted thing! Even though I am big, I have feelings like everyone else.

As I lay there feeling miserable in the snow, I began to speak. I wanted to explain what I was doing, why I had been building The Banker, how I wanted to make the world fair again. But Santa held up his hand and silenced me. I had disobeyed him. I knew I had to leave forever.

But after everyone had left and gone back

to their chores, Santa did a curious thing. He threw every cog and curve and spring from The Banker out onto the snow behind me, and he called: "This belongs to you, I think."

Now I wonder, why did he do that?

I was distraught, very sad and confused, but there was one glimmer of hope. Did he secretly agree with me? Did he think the world would be better without money? I had all the parts, so I could easily put the machine back together again. Or was he just being foolish for once in his life? After all, Santa is human, and humans, like elves, can make mistakes.

But for now I had something more urgent to think about. I was homeless and I needed to find shelter. I sprinkled some Top Grade AAA Elf Dust onto the pile of knobs and whirls and twisted metal that had been The Banker, and off I walked, knowing it would stay as mist inside my pockets until I was ready for it.

It was a long, lonely journey I embarked on, looking for a new home. Santa had stripped me of my title. Everyone had stood around to watch it happen. But as I walked, I knew in my heart of hearts I was still The Tallest Elf Of Them All.

Chapter Seven
The ShuffleBelch

So there I was, friendless and homeless, looking for a new home.

Sometimes when times are bad, I can still appreciate what small blessings are left. I felt safe, for I was strong, and in the cold mountains being a very large elf was something to be grateful for.

During my wanderings I came across something that truly made me gasp and tremble. And I did not feel so big anymore.

It was something I had thought only existed in legends. It was a ShuffleBelch worm. When I first spotted him he looked like a dark crack way up high on a white mountain. I thought perhaps it was the enormous mouth of a massive cave. I began to climb up the slope to investigate further. But then I saw that dark line in the mountains twitch and move, and I knew this was no cave I was approaching, but something perhaps far more sinister. I say perhaps because, you can never be sure, till you get to know something, what it is like. Thinking you know about someone you have never met, or that you don't like something you have never tried, is silly. Seeing that huge long dark something above you twitching way up high on the mountain slope, would you have kept on climbing, or gone back the other way? Or would you have tried to hide?

Even I, The Tallest Elf Of All, had my doubts. Carefully, I climbed higher, taking care to hide in shades of light and shadow that many creatures cannot see, for this is how elves hide best. But I did not know then that ShuffleBelches do not see, they are blind. They *feel* their prey – and hiding in shadow and light did not stop the gentle vibration of my feet on the ground.

I got closer and closer, till I could see the long bulging segments of his body, all bloated with mucous and fat. He was an enormous worm, and very quiet. I climbed around in front, higher than him now, up the slope, and saw a mouth that made my stomach churn.

It was as wide as a tree, and a complete circle of teeth, that all turned in on each other forming a tightly woven coil of fangs. I might have crept off right there and then, but looking down on him I realised he was a bit like me. He was out on a lonely mountainside, friendless, unwanted. He was big; he was different, unlike anyone else. Nobody dared to try and understand him. I could see we had that much in common. So I decided to be his friend. A friend I would not want to get too close to. These creatures eat anything that moves while they are asleep

– at least anything near enough to get caught in their foul breath and sucked in. That's the worst thing about ShuffleBelches. Their warm breath travels all the way up their long and slimy gut, through rivers of hanging fat, and they breath in hot belches that have enough force to suck you in to that circle of fangs, if you stand too close. Don't get too near a ShuffleBelch worm, for their breath and their fangs can kill you, if their burps and farts don't kill you first!

ShuffleBelches live for a few thousand years, and they sleep half their lives, in great long dream spells that can each last a hundred years or more before awakening.

I spent a long time getting to know this lonely creature, who can neither speak nor hear, but has his own way of telling his story. It turns out this ShuffleBelch was deep in the middle of one such sleep curled up inside a mountain when he was rudely awoken by a blast. It was so powerful it shook the mountain and the shaking woke him. After a yawn that lasted some weeks, he began a slow slide to the surface, to see what had awoken him. And there he felt the footfall of tiny human men putting sticks in the ground. The earth shook and fire flashed, and smoke rose into the air. They were using a human invention called dynamite, to crack open the land. And they were doing it right above him.

So the ShuffleBelch moved. He could have slid up to where the men were standing, and given them a fright. But what would have been the point? There is land enough for everyone. I have learned from watching humans that this is something most of them cannot understand. The land was here before they were born, and will be here after they are gone. In a thousand years will your name be remembered? You will soak into the land like rain. How can you own it, when it is you who'll disappear? You can't own the land. The land owns you. Some humans know this, others don't. This is what all animals understand, and elves, and goblins, and ShuffleBelches too. Only men, with their boom bam dynamite, cannot understand this.

I can tell you one thing. The ice is starting to melt. Soon we will have nowhere to live. Do you mind? What about the ferocious polar bears, the wailing wolves, the waddling penguins? They will have no home soon. All the chopping of trees and the burning of fuels to help humans get what they want, it has made the ice begin to melt because the air has got warmer. Weird, huh? But true. And sad. For with no ice mountains and bergs of white, there are no polar bears, nor Arctic wolves, nor seals, nor penguins, except maybe in human zoos – they will have to live there, and so will their children, and their children, forever, never seeing the ice again that is their home, because it is gone. Greed. That's what I wanted to stop. Greed for money is destroying our world.

Anyway, did the ShuffleBelch get mad? Did he use his greater size and strength to attack? Nope.

Despite their fearsome looks, and their terrible reputation, ShuffleBelches are a sleepy breed. They are actually most violent in their sleep, when their foul breath sucks unsuspecting food into their mouths. Awake, they would never hurt anyone.

The ShuffleBelch saw no point in trying to teach these men a thing or two. He just yawned and left his home behind to slowly whambrumble along and find somewhere else. He ended up on the lonely mountainside where I found him.

Chapter Eight
My Cave Is Carved

So there was this ShuffleBelch worm, blind and deaf, looking around for a new home in the wilderness. So I decided to help.

I walked on ahead of him, not too fast so he could keep up. He followed the tremor of my feet on the ice and snow. And I found a home for him.

It was a long thin crack, wide enough for a tall human to climb through. The stone around the crack was folded like the petals of a flower, and thick with ice. It was rather difficult for the ShuffleBelch to slide in, for he is so round and long, but his skin and fat are soft and pliable, and he wormed his way – quite literally – into the hole. Then he began to chew at the rock and ice and slowly burrowed deeper.

The tunnel of my lair was made when the ShuffleBelch slowly and casually ate his way through the stone and mud. In places he dug gradually upward, till he almost broke out onto the mountains again. In other places he dug steep pathways. It was on one such downward path that the ShuffleBelch came upon a bubble of air and water that had been enclosed inside the rock. It was home to some tiny little creatures, all covered in feathers and fur, who hopped across water and blinked brilliant lights with their eyes.

Well the ShuffleBelch came munching a hole into their world, right through from the top. The tiny creatures all turned and stared at him, and their eyes flashed. And though he was blind he hated bright lights, and so he turned and ate quickly upward again, digging a new passage with that mauling mouth of his, until he was gone from that place.

Well those little creatures blinked, and flashed, and then dived down under the water of their underground lake, and there they hid. I waited. I could smell the belching and the burping and the farting of the ShuffleBelch as he slowly munched his path further ahead.

I was fascinated by these new little creatures, so I curled up on a dark curve of stone and I waited, till up those little furry feathery critters came, and they started to skim across the water, and to sing. But their singing was a garbling sound, rather sad, and I suddenly felt they were asking me for something. What could I possibly give them? What did they need? They had been in this stone hollow for however long, a very, very, very long time and they had obviously survived. What could they need from me?

But as I sat, and as I watched, silently, I became accustomed to their looks, and I realised there were not many of them. They lived here, in their own little world away from everyone, and yet they were so few. I started to count them. It was not hard, as they came skimming across the water, or leaping high, or diving in, I got used to each one. There were five in all. Five. And I never saw any more.

I got to thinking, five is not a lot. Not if you are the only guys in your species, right? I mean, you probably have five friends, or a little less, or a few more? A lot more? Humans are everywhere. Imagine if there were only five humans in the whole world. Here was a very rare species that did not live in other places. I kind of guessed it might be true.

As Santa's Biggest Elf in charge of The Naughty List I had, over many years, gradually travelled everywhere. From ocean deep to mountain high, forest thick to desert wide, along countless trails and hidden lanes, I had never seen or heard of anything quite like them. Different. That's what they were. I liked them instantly. And even though I had been caught building The Banker, and thrown out by Santa, and stripped of my title Santa's Biggest Elf, and I was now deep in a tunnel under some mountains following an enormous farting worm, I found that I was smiling.

I headed off after that ShuffleBelch again and found that he had munched a kind of circular route back through the rock and ice. Now there was an upward slope that led away from the lake, but if you followed it, as I did, you reached the very place where he had first munched downward and bitten into the bubble, into the private little world where those bright eyed creatures lived.

Following the tunnel, I went straight past the hole again then carried on higher and higher, till I found a spot where indeed the ShuffleBelch had stopped eating, and simply fallen asleep.

And as usual, the creature had turned back on himself, so his mouth, with its hundreds of sharp teeth that formed a tight circle of snoring fangs, was pointed back in the way he had come. This was for the purposes of feeding.

ShuffleBelches, as you now know, sleep very long and very deep, and can be in dreams for a hundred or more of your human years at a time. And though they have no eyes, so cannot see, and no ears, so cannot hear, they feel the vibrations of anything that comes walking or slithering or leaping toward them. And anything unfortunate enough to come close enough can get sucked into the interlacing fangs as the ShuffleBelch snores deeply.

I thought I had better make a sign, so I did. Using my newly grown claws I etched out a sign. In case anyone should come stumbling into the sleeping ShuffleBelch by mistake.

"Keep Out. Go No Further. Or you shall be swallowed by the ShuffleBelch. By Order Of...

I stopped scratching the words. Who should I say 'By Order Of' from? Such words made the reader sit up and listen. Surely it had to be By Order Of someone? I was not Santa's Biggest Elf anymore. I could have clawed 'By Order Of GobDrop, The Tallest Elf Of Them All.' But what was an elf doing here, so deep below the mountains anyway? Readers might not take it seriously. Then an idea struck me. It was only the ShuffleBelch, and the little critters in the lake with the blinking eyes, and me, down here. Or was there someone else? I could make myself king. Why not? Just for fun? Would anyone mind? And as soon as I thought it, I smiled and clawed it in. 'By Order Of GobDrop The Goblin, King Under The Snows.'

I made that whole long tunnel my home. I shared it happily with the sleeping ShuffleBelch, and the blinking creatures in their lake. Who were they? I wanted to give them a name. It's because of the garbling warble of their song that I called them GarbleWarbles.

Chapter Nine
My Machine Lives Again

I checked out the whole tunnel and decided that the best place to rebuild The Banker was right in that spot where the worm had turned. Right beside that hole that fell through to the lake. Right beside it, or right above it?

Then I began to wonder. Was it food that the GarbleWarbles were asking for in their sad little song? Peering down that hole I could see the flashing lights of those little creatures all the way down there in their gigantic pool. And I wondered, would they eat money?

Well money is a human thing. No other animal in the earthly kingdom uses the stuff. I mean pets do, but it's not conscious. It's their human owners who spend money on them. Did you ever see a dog, cat, parrot, or goldfish counting out money, or handing over change? Nope. Money is a human thing. But maybe, just maybe, these little guys were hungry, and maybe, just maybe, money would help fill their bellies. So I pulled the mist that was the broken parts of The Banker out of my pocket. I also found to my surprise the pinch of Elf Invisibility dust and one page of The Naughty List that had been in my pocket all this time as well. I had forgotten I had even put it in there. It was the page with the idea on it, about the boy who sucked up all his parents' money. That's the only page I ever took, even though elves now say I stole The Naughty List. They say it is the worst thing I have ever done. Maybe it is. Well it was just one page, and I did not steal it, but took it away by accident.

So I rebuilt The Banker – that long and twisted machine, with its long funnel and its huge magnet and its massive pump. I poked the magnetic end of it out of the hole in the ice, just to try it out. And once The Banker was chuffing and puffing and bamrumbeling with life, I waited till it was full of magnetised money – sucked in from every corner of the globe – and I pushed a big red button that said OUT and opened its enormous mouth. The money fell down like snow into the hole below.

I sprang on those long legs of mine from tunnel wall to tunnel roof, hip hopping along the scooping tunnel that the worm had eaten, to get to the shore of the lake and find out what would happen. As I arrived the first notes settled on the water. All was silent. All was still. There were no waves. Not even a ripple. More notes fell. Nothing happened.

Then it began. I heard a single 'pop' as a small mouth poked up above the water and tasted the strange papery leaves. Then there was another 'pop' and then another. Pop, pop pop, pop, pop. The GarbleWarbles were nibbling at the notes, opening their mouths wide and sucking them right in. They were eating the money – and they liked it!

Those little guys kept The Banker busy. Their number was so small, just five, and I hoped that by feeding them, they would grow stronger, and have teeny weeny GarbleWarble babies, and thus multiply.

I was like their dad, or their guardian. I kept a close eye on them, and every time more were born, I would scratch into the cave wall how many there were. I was so happy to see more and more of them.

I kept The Banker working night and day. As its mighty engine roared like a dragon with belly ache, the teeth of the machine would open and drop those notes down. The GarbleWarbles would skip across the lake's surface, eyes all ashimmer with light: blink, blink, blink.

They were my only company in that cave, except for the sleeping ShuffleBelch.

I got used to being alone in that cave, while in the outside world the elves told fearsome tales about me, and the stories about me changed and shifted until they were legends, and everyone was afraid of my name.

I knew nobody would ever know the truth about me, or even care. I had been told by Santa to go where no elf would ever see me, and I had. I would always sit alone by my fire at the cave entrance, with no one to keep me company.

Then one day, my new little friend appeared. Not SnowSlime – sorry, I mean SnowShine. No, it was a soft white Arctic hare that came to my cave first. It was RuffinMuffin.

He was, like all hares, courageous, sweet and wise. He had always admired me quietly when I was Santa's Biggest Elf, and had watched on sadly the day Santa threw me out. It must have taken great courage for the hare to leave Santa's Lodge, all alone, and wander into the mountains to seek me out. He had tried and tried to find me, and he was the first who did, long before I found SnowShine wandering alone.

As RuffinMuffin sat by my fire that first

night he arrived, he described the terrible tales the big elves were telling the small elves about The Christmas Goblin.

I shuddered. It's not nice when people are gossiping about you. But RuffinMuffin never believed any of their stories. He was worried that I was lonely and sad. We became inseparable. Fluffy RuffinMuffin the Arctic hare became my white shadow. Wherever I was, he was near. He was my only companion beside the fire and as I hunted, or walked along the tunnel to The Banker. Which suited him, for he was terribly shy. I don't think he ever showed himself to SnowShine, did he? At least he never said a thing to SnowShine, not until right toward the end of our story.

I am sure SnowShine told you – when he arrived near my cave, lost in the white mountains, how I bagged him up and took him in. I treated him pretty well. Sure I called him SnowSlime and spoke in nasty riddles to keep him scared. Remember though, he was an elf, and elves had decided to shun me and make up terrible tales.

I thought that one elf is like another, and no elf would ever do anything to help me. But I was wrong. Not all elves are the same. Not all of anything is the same, no matter what colour skin or what type of hair it has or what it sounds like when it speaks. SnowSlime – I mean SnowShine – had the most annoying squeaky voice I have ever heard. Arrrghhh! But he was small and vulnerable and needed a safe place to stay. It takes time to find out what lies inside. I was to learn SnowShine is different, and not just because he was small.

Was I mean to him? Not really. Sure I gave him a nasty name. And I got the little guy to do some chores for me. But he was staying in my place. Fair is fair. SnowShine never went hungry. He had a roof to keep out hail and snow and freezing wind. A little bit of sweeping never hurt anyone.

SnowShine got lots of good things from me. Food. A roof. A warm fire. Even if he did not like the way I hung him up from a hook over the flames. The kid was still warm, wasn't he? Because something happened, after he had been living with me a while. I needed his help. And he had to be thunderbulbously naughty and superfabulistically brave to help me.

This is what SnowShine didn't tell you – the elves had laid a trap for me!

Chapter Ten
The Elf Trap

It began when I brewed up that Goblin Storm to catch the bag of Christmas songs. Why did I do that? Not everyone likes Christmas carols. Take me for example, back in the days when I was still Santa's Biggest Elf, living at Santa's Lodge.

Whenever there was a choir evening, in the Great Hall filled with thousands of elves, amid the glow of lights dancing along the stone walls, I would stand silent and out of sight. And since I was Santa's Biggest Elf, nobody dared tell me I had to join in. I do like music, I just can't stand soft and soggy carols.

With that magical bag, Santa was trying to make sure that everyone joined in, whether they liked Christmas songs or not. The whole idea behind that bag was just wrong. Let those who love songs hear them, and those who do not, let them go without. Santa was planning to take that bag everywhere, to everyone. I had to try and put a stop to it, don't you see? To me that day, the sound coming from The Sleigh was even worse than usual. I was fed up with the roll of Santa's laugh as he called to the reindeer from far overhead. That was bad enough. But the racket coming from his sleigh that day was much worse. I couldn't stand the sound of those Christmas carols. RuffinMuffin was there in the snow behind me, and he hated it too and was twitching his ears in frustration

When I heard those carols drifting down across the mountains toward us, I had to do something. I mean how loud does Santa need to play his music? I wanted to make sure nobody ever heard such a racket again.

Sometimes, when you know both sides to a story, you might just change your mind.

I took a big risk brewing up that storm because it helped the elves know where I was hiding. I'm sure they had all heard such bad things about me. RuffinMuffin told me they wanted me gone. No elf ever stopped to hear my side of the story. No elf? That's not quite true. SnowShine did, though it took him a while to start to understand.

Chapter Eleven
Snow Rest For The Wicked

The day Santa found my cave, little RuffinMuffin was out in the snow. He had wandered alongside me as I hunted for food. I was very close to a pack of tasty wolves when Santa's Sleigh suddenly appeared.

I am ashamed to say that in my rush to beat Father Christmas to my cave, I forgot all about my little hare friend. I left him there near the wolves and they began to circle around him. They had been hunted, now they were the hunters. Only when that dratted song bag refused to burn, and Santa stood there in the mouth of my cave, with all his reindeer glaring in too, did I see RuffinMuffin was in trouble.

I caught sight of him through the gap between Santa's boots. He was way off down the valley, with those wolves chasing after him. I forgot all about the bag! I called for the others to help and slipped off between Santa's boots to save my little mate.

Well hares are quick, but so are wolves, and in that wild chase they all ran as fast as they could, with RuffinMuffin leaping away from them, and the wolves bounding after him.

No one is faster than me on the ice. As an elf I was always good on my feet, able to climb to places that humans never could reach. But as you know, when the machine steamed and belched and burbled and bubbled, I started to change. My elf legs became springy and spidery. And they grew claws that can slice into hard ice like a knife sliding into soft butter. They might not win a beauty contest, but my claws rule the slopes of this vast icy land.

Terrified for my friend's life, I scrambled and pounced across the valley walls and I caught up with those wolves just in time. As soon as they caught sight of me they ran off with a hungry howl. I could have given chase and caught one, for I was hungry too. But little RuffinMuffin just collapsed on the snow trembling with fright, so I bundled him up against my warm green and purple fur and cuddled him close.

It took a while for him to stop shaking and I just sat there, below a cliff of perilous ice, holding him so that he knew he was safe. Then, when he was ready, we set off together across the snow.

Chapter Twelve
Snared By Elven Thread

But what I did not know is that as soon as Santa got the bag of Christmas songs, and lifted SnowShine into The Sleigh, and off they flew, the elves stayed in the mountains and got themselves busy. They set a trap – for me. Sentries with bows stood hidden in many of the higher crags.

Elven archers are the best bowmen in the world. Their bows can fire arrows through whole mountains. Those guards watched as only elves can but they saw no sign of me. They need not have bothered. I was sat there comforting the terrified RuffinMuffin while the real trap was set.

I sat there cuddling the hare and watched as Santa's Sleigh disappeared with SnowShine and the pesky bag of carols sat right there inside it. I did not care about the songs anymore. At least I had saved RuffinMuffin's life. But I was sad to see the little elf go. Sad but glad too. He was going home, and he would not be ignored anymore. Now Santa's tiniest elf would be a somebody. He had saved the bag of Christmas songs. I was sad to see him go, but I was glad for him.

And as I sat there feeling lonely, and cuddling little RuffinMuffin who had almost lost his life, those elven archers stood high up in the mountains watching out for me, while other elves got busy. They climbed the heights and built an enormous web, shaped like a spider's, made of invisible Elven Thread. They used ten miles of thread to set the trap. It stretched between one craggy peak to another, and hugged the mountain side, just three valleys away from my home.

Once RuffinMuffin had calmed down, we set off hunting again. I went along one valley, then the next, hunting for food, with the hare shadowing me, and I found something out there in the wilderness all right: a thin strand of Elven Thread.

The unexpected strand caught fast around my legs as I was leaping across a cliff of ice. I teetered in mid air and fell hard onto my face. Suddenly there was more thread gripping my arms and my fur and my head. I thrashed with my legs. My claws cut through it and for a moment I thought I would be alright. I tried to stand, but the thread around those long legs of mine grew tighter. I clawed and kicked but the thread creaked and whined, it whipped back on me like a lasso. My claws slashed and I could hear thread after thread snap. But the more I slashed and bit and cut the more the long web of thread looped around me.

The last thing I saw was RuffinMuffin turn his white cotton tail and leap away up the mountain. Even my little friend had deserted me, just after I had saved him. The sadness of that took away all my strength. I just collapsed, as the Elven Thread tangled about me so tight it turned daylight into night.

Then came a gentle whistle that was so subtle it would be impossible for human ears to hear. It was the sound of elven arrows, singing as they spun through the air. And when elven arrows sing, there is always a spell. The arrow tips hit me like shards of stinging rain, and a deep Elven Sleep spell soaked into my blood. In moments, I was out cold.

I awoke to a noise like the breathing of a dragon. And there was a smell, foul and sickly, everywhere. My eyes opened wide, but I could see nothing, or at least, not much. Only a crack. And through that crack I saw... I closed my eyes, surely not? I opened them again. It was the round, fanged mouth of the ShuffleBelch that I could spy through the crack of my Elven Thread prison.

While I was sleeping under their spell, the elves had explored my cave. They'd found the place where the trail split in two. They found the sweet little GarbleWarbles, and they found the sign: "Keep Out. Go No Further. Or you shall be swallowed by the ShuffleBelch. By Order of GobDrop The King Under The Snows."

That gave them an idea. A very nasty one. Can you guess what it was?

Here I was, GobDrop, The Tallest Elf Of Them All, The King Under The Snows, greatest of the hunters, champion of The Naughty List, tied upon in Elven Thread about to be fed to my sleeping friend. I tried to kick and roll about, to shake the Thread loose, or make a big enough tremor to wake the ShuffleBelch up. Surely, if he was awake, if he knew somehow it was me, I would not get eaten?

But my attempts were futile. With every thrash and kick and claw the Elven Thread grew tighter. And it muffled any vibration I might have made against the ground. The ShuffleBelch stayed deep in his dream, with that revolting fart breath of his sucking in, out, in, out.

There in the darkness I tried to find an end to the Elven Thread that bound me. If I could just find the end, maybe I could pull the whole bundle free?

It was useless. It was just too big a tangle. I closed my eyes and trembled. In the whole of the North Pole, among all those lonely mountains and vast plains of shimmering white, there was no one living thing that cared enough to save me. And even if anyone had wanted too, nobody could!

While I had been dreaming, Santa and SnowShine were flying around the world singing songs and giving out presents. I awoke at about the time SnowShine returned to Santa's Lodge. It was his first time back since leaving, without permission, to climb the mountain. Everyone wanted to see him and ask him all about his adventures. SnowShine, Santa's Smallest Elf, was suddenly a somebody! And then came the news, he was going to receive a Santa Award, in front of everyone, from The Big Man, Father Christmas, himself.

Well the whole of Santa's Lodge went SnowShine crazy. Flags of starlight were hung along the corridors, with his name printed on them. Cakes were baked and printed with elaborate designs of his face. Poets wrote poems about him. Artists drew portraits of him. Minstrels sang songs about him. Everyone knew SnowShine now. And nobody wanted to miss the excitement of watching Santa's Smallest Elf receive his Santa Award. Every set of eyes in Santa's kingdom gathered to watch as Father Christmas placed that 'Santa's Bravest Elf' badge on SnowShine's jacket. Then every pair of ears heard Santa's cherry and mistletoe voice saying:

"SnowShine, you are small on the outside, but tall as a mountain on the inside."

And everyone saw that little elf's gigantic grin.

Did I say everyone from Santa's kingdom had gathered to watch and listen? Well that's not quite true. I certainly wasn't enjoying the party. I was still trapped in my prison of Elven Thread. The ShuffleBelch hadn't been invited either. He was still fast asleep in front of me. The elves who were my captors knew nothing about the celebrations. And as for the GarbleWarbles, well, Santa and his helpers didn't know that any such thing as a GarbleWarble even existed. My friend RuffinMuffin wasn't at the party when it started, but, as you will soon find out, he arrived later.

Chapter Thirteen
A Word In Your Ear

The hubble and bubble and ballyhoo of the celebrations were still going strong when one very tired SnowShine sat himself down on a crystal chair. It had been carved for him, and his name was right there in bold letters across the back. Now that was a privilege!

There the little elf sat, as the bigger elves polished his boots and brushed his hair, when suddenly someone came hopping in through the door. It was the white hare from GobDrop's cave. SnowShine saw him at once, since the hare was no longer camouflaged against a background of white snow.

SnowShine noticed that the hare seemed agitated. He was hopping frantically this way and that between the larger elves' feet. He was doing a strange little dance, rolling his eyes and flapping his long white ears. Santa's Smallest Elf gave a wave of his hand and the other larger elves stepped away. The hare leapt up onto the chair, then whispered something in SnowShine's ear, so quietly that nobody else, not even other elves, could hear.

"Psst, psst, psst! Elven archers have caught GobDrop. He's in a tangled web of Elven Thread. They are going to feed him to the ShuffleBelch."

Now I bet SnowShine never told you anything about *that*, did he? He kept this part of our story secret. But any story always has two sides, and some stories have many. And usually there are holes where things have been left unsaid, or said wrong, or deliberately hidden.

Well, SnowShine had only been wearing his new Santa Award badge for one day. This was a high honour and everyone in Santa's Lodge noticed him. Remember in the beginning of my story, many of you thought that I, GobDrop, was not worth knowing? Now you know more, do you think I am worth saving? If you were SnowShine would you go and help me? What if Santa found out and took away your Santa Award? Would you still try to save me then?

SnowShine leapt straight up and went to tell Santa. He knew that Santa would never allow the elves to do something unkind to another creature. Surely if he found out, The Big Man would stop this happening. But when he reached the door to Santa's Private Apartments, he saw a sign hanging across the door. 'Santa Is

Sleeping. Do Not Disturb!'

Hmmmmm. SnowShine hoped Santa had just hung up that sign a moment ago, and was maybe still awake. But he decided that he'd better not knock. Or ring. Or whistle. For such a thing might wake The Big Man, and that would be against Santa's rules. He took a quick peek through Santa's window. But all he saw were the curtains drawn, and a rather odd looking hare with crooked ears sitting on the windowsill.

SnowShine knew that there was no time to waste. He made his excuses to the other elves – telling a few little lies about needing time to rest, and to please not disturb him after such a long adventure. And now he was someone important, everyone listened, and everyone left him alone. And once all elven ears and eyes were somewhere else, SnowShine slipped quietly out of Santa's Lodge.

SnowShine did not know the way to my cave. He'd only stumbled across me that first time by getting lost. When he came back, in Santa's Sleigh, he was so full of delight he never bothered to notice. But RuffinMuffin knew the way so the elf followed the hare. It is a long and steep and tiring journey at the best of times but it seemed all the longer, and all the steeper, because both hare and elf wanted to do it quickly. They wanted to stop the Christmas Goblin being fed to the ShuffleBelch. Would they get there in time?

Once they crossed the last icy crag, they looked down towards the cave. They could not see the entrance at all. But they knew it lay hidden there among endless shimmering white. What they did see were the elf sentries armed with bows guarding the cave. Would you have tried to get past them?

SnowShine knew there was no way they would fire their arrows at him, but they might stop him going in, because he was so small. He might be all-important back at Santa's Lodge, but these elves didn't know that. For a moment his heart faltered, and the little elf almost did not dare take up his courage and walk straight toward those guards.

But then he puffed out his chest, threw his head back to look as important as he could, and swelling his chest to show off his Santa's Bravest Elf badge he walked straight past the sentries, giving them a light salute as he did so.

SnowShine followed RuffinMuffin along the winding tunnel until it got to that place where the tunnel parted. One way went up and the other way went down. RuffinMuffin hopped on up the hill, straight past the sign that read: 'You shall be swallowed by the ShuffleBelch.'

SnowShine took a deep breath. He had never gone that way before. But the little elf had more important things on his mind than his safety, and so up the slope, past the sign, he went. He knew what lay ahead. An enormous worm that could neither see nor hear nor smell, but would feel the vibration of his feet as he walked across the floor — for even the light foot tread of Santa's tiniest elves cannot escape the twitching whiskers of a ShuffleBelch. SnowShine knew that the worm ahead was enormous, with a mouth like a tunnel bristling with fangs. Would you have followed the hare past the sign and up into the foul smelling darkness?

For dark it was, as the tunnel looped around into shadow. And as they journeyed further, a thick and foul stench settled in the air. Every now and then SnowShine could hear a deep gurgling belch or a stringy stretched out fart, coming from the dreaded beast ahead. The smell and the worm's breath made the little elf's tummy start to retch.

SnowShine might have stopped there. Lying to the elves to save GobDrop was one thing. And crossing those perilous mountains had been hard enough. But the stench from the sleeping worm was the single worst thing the little elf had ever come across. Tears welled in his eyes and his tongue began to stick in his mouth. His nostrils tried to close up on themselves like glue. The elf knew what the legend said. Get too close to a ShuffleBelch and its horrid breath will suck you into a circle of pointed teeth.

Did SnowShine, Santa's Smallest Elf, turn back and return to the safety of Santa's Lodge? He did. But not yet. For SnowShine knew that if there was one thing that Santa's Smallest Elf was really good at, it was unraveling Elven Thread. It was the one thing he was best at in the whole world. And right now that was what I, GobDrop, needed him to do.

Did I ask him to risk his life for me? No. How could I? I was knotted and tied in my prison of Thread. I could not even click my tongue, let alone speak. I knew I had reached the end of my days, and would soon just be a lump in the belly of a worm.

Imagine my surprise when I suddenly saw my little white hare friend hop into view. He was stood just to the side of that terrible mouth, and I could see the warm breath of the ShuffleBelch ruffling his fur. I raised my eyebrows and tried to warn him, but I could not speak. Then imagine my amazement as I saw a tiny hand reaching forward, two fingers in an open pinch moving this way and that, choosing just the right place, and just the right moment. And then, suddenly the whole twisted prison of tight Elven Thread fell loosely around me into a heap on the floor. There, before my startled eyes stood SnowShine, Santa's Smallest Elf, with the end of the Elven Thread between his fingertips.

Well, we ran from that dark and foul smelling place and then we stopped. There were elves at the cave entrance. And perhaps there were others patrolling the cave? I reached into my pockets and felt the tiny sprinkle of invisibility dust. Would it be enough to disguise me, SnowShine, and RuffinMuffin? I hoped it would. I covered us all the best I could. Only tiny patches of us were still visible, a hair here, a patch of fur there. If we were ever so quiet, perhaps we could creep past those alert eleven guards?

Well for SnowShine on his tiny elven feet, and RuffinMuffin on his soft padded paws, it was easy. But I had my long claws that went click, click, click on the ground.

We went to the lake, wondering at each turn if we would come across some guards. We turned that tight bend past the lake and walked straight down that slope, our hearts beating fast and hard. The water appeared before us, and we picked up some half-eaten notes of human money, and held it up in our hands. Immediately a GarbleWarble leapt out of the lake and came skimming towards us. The GarbleWarbles trusted me and the little fluffy feathery critter leapt straight into my claws.

I made my claws into a little prison and carried him along. I did not like doing this but we needed his singing to hide the click of my claws. And sure enough, the further we took him from the lake, the louder he sang that mournful wail, and suddenly those elven guards heard it and they came running. We pressed ourselves up against the tunnel walls, and put the little critter down. When the guards saw him lying there on the ground singing, they rubbed their chins and wondered how he got there, but they were kindly and carried him back to the lake. While they were busy doing this, we slipped away.

Chapter Fourteen
Badge of Honour

Once we had climbed high into the mountains beyond, we stopped, and I blew the Elf Invisibility dust away. Only when we were safe did SnowShine surprise me again. He took off that shiny new 'Santa's Bravest Elf' badge and tried to give it to me.

RuffinMuffin had told him everything, as they had crossed the mountains on their way to rescue me. SnowShine now knew I was really The Tallest Elf Of Them All. He said he had always wanted to meet me. And now the hare had told him what I had wanted to do – take money off the humans so that The Naughty List would work. He thought that I was The Bravest Elf Of All. He wanted me to have the badge.

He felt bad that Santa had given it to him, because he had broken Santa's rules, and he had left The Lodge again without permission. The little elf said that he did not deserve the badge because if anyone knew he had saved GobDrop the Goblin, they would be very, very cross and decide to take it away from him.

So he wanted me to have that badge. What do you think I said?

"Keep it SnowShine," I laughed. "You deserve it, for saving my life and setting me free."

So Santa's Smallest Elf, saved me, The Tallest Elf Of Them All. I would never have seen that coming. And it taught me to never judge anyone by their looks again. I was mean to him when he first arrived at my cave because he was just a squeaky-voiced elf. But now I know better. I decided never to bully little guys again – you never know when you might need them. Where did I go after that? Well that's for me, and RuffinMuffin, and SnowShine, to know. It's our little secret. We all have a little secret or two – even Santa himself.

Author's dedication:

'To my first grandson, Kai Harley Peacefull-Day, who emerged into this world as this tale was being written. May life hold you gently, and may sweet laughter never be far from your lips.'

Adrian Beckingham, (A.K.A. The Man from Story Mountain) is a leading story-teller who has spun magical tales at the British Museum, Glastonbury Festival and venues across the globe. An active advocate for the power of story to transform and heal, Adrian is well known for his work using stories to improve mental health in community care arenas. He was also founding chairman of The Siddhartha Foundation, a charity establishing a residential school for Himalayan orphans in Kathmandu city.

Also by Adrian Beckingham:

Stories That Crafted The Earth
ISBN: 9780906362655

A unique collection of ancient stories gathered from cultures around the globe. They tell of how the world's first hills, mountains, forests, rivers, oceans, animals and people were formed.

The King of the Things
ISBN: 978-1-906132-50-7

www.themanfromstorymountain.org.uk

The King Of The Things

by Adrian Beckingham

Hunch was different from everyone else. He knew it. They knew it. And his arch rival Tax, who was the best at absolutely everything, never failed to use it against him. However, nobody knew a surprise was at hand, from the Things that lurked deep inside the wood. Things so strange that nobody has ever been able to describe them!

'It shows what is right or wrong, what is unfair or fair, and kind or horrible in a creative and magical way.It's an unusual story, told from the heart, that stops people judging by looks and knowing that what is important is what's inside people's hearts. If you're someone who likes to be different, you need to read The King of Things.'
Treya (Age 11, nearly 12!)

ISBN: 978-1-906132-50-7

Order from: www.mogzilla.co.uk/shop

Lightning Source UK Ltd.
Milton Keynes UK
UKOW03f1515211113

221553UK00001B/4/P